Going Through the Gate

Janet S. Anderson

Going Through the Gate

Dutton Children's Books • New York

Library of Congress Cataloging-in-Publication Data
Anderson, Janet S.
Going through the gate / by Janet S. Anderson.—1st ed.
p.   cm.
Summary: The five sixth-grade students in a small town
prepare for their teacher's annual graduation ceremony, a
mysterious ritual that several generations of students have
experienced but no one can discuss.
ISBN 0-525-45836-0 (hc)
[1. Teachers—Fiction. 2. Identity—Fiction. 3. Animals—
Fiction. 4. Supernatural—Fiction.] I. Title.
PZ7.A5366Go 1997 [Fic]—dc21 97-15227 CIP AC

Published in the United States by Dutton Children's Books,
a division of Penguin Books USA Inc.
375 Hudson Street, New York, New York 10014

Designed by Semadar Megged
Printed in USA   First Edition
10 9 8 7 6 5 4 3 2 1

FOR MY PARENTS
AND FOR TONY

One

It was a Sunday night, almost summer, with a cool breeze that lifted the light curtains at bedroom windows gently and sporadically. It was a perfect night for sleeping, and Miss Clough didn't sleep at all.

ↄ ↄ ↄ

Becky slept until her clock ticked over to six. She lay quietly for a few minutes, watching the lighted dial with satisfaction. It really did work, what Miss Clough had taught them. Imagine a clock just behind your eyes, set the time, and then pull it deep into the blackness inside your head. At the right hour, you will reel yourself up out of sleep like a fish out of deep water.

So she could get that part right. And she'd worked hard with her chickadee. In a few minutes it would flit down onto her windowsill, snatch a sunflower seed, and dart with it to the safety of the honeysuckle. Back and forth, back and forth, its black eyes bright, used now to her silent presence on the other side of the window. For weeks, Becky had watched and listened and pushed herself to imagine bark beneath a claw, the itch of pinfeathers coming in, the pull of wings lifting into the sky.

But imagining was one thing. Knowing was another. Did she really *know*, know enough for what would happen today on the other side of the gate? She shivered now in the cool dawn. "Going through the gate." That's what people called it in town when, every few years, someone disappeared. Standing around the post office, the hardware store, their voices would be low and serious. "Gil? Well, he just hasn't been himself since that bad thing with his family, since getting laid off, since getting so sick. They say he left a note. They say he went through the gate."

Well, today, she'd go through the gate. And she was scared. What if it didn't work for her and she didn't graduate? She looked over at the bulk of her older sister Nancy just stirring in the other bed. She wished she could ask how it had happened for her two years ago, before she'd started taking the bus to the junior high and its world of homework and after-school clubs and basketball games.

But Nancy wouldn't tell her. She couldn't, just as Dad couldn't, just as no one could who'd gone through Miss Clough's sixth grade in the last one-room school in the county. What happened at graduation changed your life and it was yours, only yours, until the day you died.

❧ ❧ ❧

Eddy, as usual, slept soundly, not getting up until his normal set time of seven. Eddy didn't have to observe nature in the wild. Many true frogs, *Ranidae*, were perfectly happy living indoors, as long as you gave them a large-enough terrarium and an ample food supply. And Eddy didn't worry that he didn't know enough. He'd been studying frogs for seven years now, ever since he was in kindergarten and Miss Clough had had them all collect tadpoles at the town-line pond.

He'd watched them breathlessly over the next couple of months, spending every free minute at the ten-gallon tank in the back of the room. Observing them change, seeing their tails disappear and their legs emerge, being there when the first tiny frog crawled from the water up onto the waiting rock. . . . That frog had been the most satisfying sight of his life.

It still was. Sometimes, forced outside with his father and brothers to "play," dropping balls, stumbling through games with incomprehensible rules, he'd think *why?* Why can tadpoles do it and not people? What if he . . . if people knew that what they were now wasn't them? Knew that they'd change, that their bodies that didn't fit anywhere, couldn't do anything, would one day, no question about it, crawl up out of the water and be . . . perfect. Strong, powerful, handsome . . . perfect. Then it wouldn't matter when other people laughed at everything you said and everything you did, at what you looked like and what you wore.

But that was silly. A silly idea, a silly question. Not a question a scientist would ask. Scientists asked about facts. Scientists studied how things are. Like family, genus, species . . . size, color, life span, habits. He'd gone over it all last night after he'd turned out his light. Of course, he'd have preferred *Rana catesbeiana*. That was his first choice, the bullfrog, king of frogs in the northern United States. But Miss Clough had said no. *Rana pipiens*, the smaller leopard frog, was better, she'd said, both for him and for the group.

That was okay. He didn't know exactly how he felt about Miss Clough, but he knew he trusted her. Miss Clough knew how important frogs were and had given him a key to the school so that he could stay late to study the journals and books that seemed to appear just in the order he needed them. He trusted Miss Clough and knew today at graduation he'd be given something that herpetologists three times his age couldn't even dream of. And something else? For a second he allowed himself to think how it would be, how it would *feel*. Then he pushed it away, pulled on his clothes and went downstairs for his usual big breakfast.

ㄱ   ㄱ   ㄱ

Penny never ate breakfast. It wasn't that she wasn't hungry in the morning. By recess she was always so starved that she'd gobble down everything in her lunch box and then have to wait until after school to eat again, unless Becky had brought something to share with her at noon, which she usually did. No, she just didn't have time for breakfast. It was always hard to wake up, now that her mother had to work and the house was so quiet, and then she had to fix her hair and put on her makeup and wipe just the right amount off so Miss Clough wouldn't give her one of those looks out of her bottomless black eyes. Then she had to decide what to wear, because the outfit she'd laid out the night before never looked quite right the next morning and so usually she had to iron a new blouse or find the right earrings, the ones that really fit how she looked today.

And today she wanted to look especially good, even though Miss Clough had told them to wear old clothes, but how could you wear old clothes when today was graduation? Not the graduation where all the parents came and maybe even her father if he wasn't mad at her for once, and if the truck company that had finally hired him after his accident let him. Not the graduation that was really just a party so it really didn't matter who came, but *the* graduation, their special private once-in-a-lifetime graduation. Just Miss Clough and the five of them, she and Becky and Eddy and Mary Margaret and Tim.

Tim. Penny brushed her hair harder, thinking of Tim and his soft blond hair and his hard blue eyes and his sullenness, so different from the boys Penny had known all her life, even the older boys who were in junior high and high school, who had begun looking at her now when they passed her on the road, looking out of the corners of their eyes and then looking away again. Tim never looked away. His eyes challenged her, challenged her to hate the stupid little town and the stupid little school as much as he had from the minute he'd arrived late last December.

Late. It was getting late, and Penny still had to

put on her dress, the bright red, cardinal-red dress she'd bought just for today, bought with months of saved allowance and babysitting money. Her first choice had been blue jay, because blue was her favorite color and jays were loud and restless and full of life, but Miss Clough had chosen cardinal instead. Still, she'd agreed on a male cardinal. Penny didn't have to be the female, the dull pinky-beige female that kept to the shadows and looked so boring. Sex didn't matter, Miss Clough had said, and it had been hard for Penny not to laugh. Of course sex didn't matter to Miss Clough, who was old and who had never married and whose dresses hung on her lately like old sacks.

Penny gave herself one last look in the mirror and then opened her new red lipstick one more time. There. And she wasn't going to wipe any of it off. Not today. Not for anybody.

ﭐ   ﭐ   ﭐ

Tim almost didn't get up at all. He'd snuck out again the night before, which hadn't been hard. It never was. His aunt and uncle always went to bed at nine on Sundays, right after their favorite TV show, and by ten the house was dead. The town was dead, too, but at least Tim was out in it, not cooped up in that little room behind the kitchen that used to be full of stuff nobody wanted anymore.

Tim had to laugh. It still was, in a way. Because who wanted him? Not his aunt and uncle, who'd never had kids, and who drove him crazy even when he knew they were trying to be nice. Not his mother, who'd disappeared when Tim was three, and whom he hardly remembered. And his father? His father, who'd always been his best pal? Well, last fall his best pal had decided to get married again, and Sheila had three little kids who took up all the room in her crummy apartment. And Timmy boy, until they can get together enough cash to rent a bigger place, you are out of luck.

So Tim had snuck out last night and ridden his bike up and down all the back roads around town, skittering through gravel and potholes until he was so tired he figured he'd have to be able to sleep. And he had slept, but not enough, and his sleep had been full of dreams, dreams of small animals rustling through leaves and birds flocking down onto huge meadows, screaming, to feed.

Miss Clough. She was to blame for dreams like that. She was crazy. There was no doubt in Tim's mind that she was crazy as a loon. If Tim scared easily, he'd be terrified thinking about what Miss Clough thought she was going to pull off today. But of course he wasn't scared. It was all garbage, even though he'd figured he'd better go along with the routine. It saved trouble. So he'd come up with his two choices and hadn't even complained when Miss Clough dumped the first. It figured.

No, he'd been a good little boy and accepted what she'd said. He'd brought home "for study" the stuffed brook trout she'd taken from her collection in the back of the room. He'd even made a couple of trips to the creek to "observe," although he'd spent most of the time there smoking the cigarettes he'd filched from his uncle and thinking about Penny. Penny was okay. At least she wasn't half bad looking and she had some guts and she knew what it was like not having your father around.

"Tim? Timmy? Better get up! You don't want to be late today!"

Oh, yeah, not today. Well, he'd get up and he'd go and, yeah, he'd go through whatever junk Miss

Clough put them through to "graduate." Except maybe he'd surprise her, just a little bit. Because it hadn't been trout he'd been "observing" down under the bridge. Not trout at all.

ˎ ˎ ˎ

Mary Margaret hated Sundays. No, of course she didn't hate Sundays. That would be a sin. It was just that Sundays were so long. That Sunday she'd been up at dawn, as always. As always she'd gotten the five "oldies" breakfasted and washed and dressed for church while her mother fussed with the "newie," little Colleen. At seven months, Colleen was still a baby, still perfect. Mary Margaret had known for a long time that although her mother would have said she loved them all, all her children equally, she loved them best during that short, short time before they could toddle away from her, get into dirt or mischief, or talk back.

So that Sunday, like all Sundays, Mary Margaret had watched the others during the long afternoon, while her mother rested. She'd kept nine-year-old John from killing Danny, both of them from killing Bridget, and two-year-old Kathleen from killing herself. Joey, who was ten, had gone home with Gram after church, and Mary Margaret had been more grateful than she could say that he wasn't around. He would have helped her, tried at least to help her, but he would have wanted to talk, too. Mary Margaret was the only person he *could* talk to—she knew that—but talking to Joey, connecting with Joey, would have forced her to think about how much he needed her. She didn't want to think about that. She didn't want to think about anything. She had just wanted to get through the day. Just one more day.

Like every Sunday, after chores, after supper, had come what her father called family time. Mary Margaret wondered if he knew how much she hated family time. No, not hated, of course not hated, but how with its loud games and music and laughter it was something for which at twelve she was far too old. Far, far too old.

But of course he didn't know. Nobody knew. Just as nobody knew the secret that she'd hugged to herself for almost eight months. It was hers, and no one else would ever know. Ever. Not even after tomorrow.

And Sunday had finally ended. It always did. And, after everyone had been washed and read to and settled, Mary Margaret had gone to bed. She'd had only a second to remember swallows darting graceful and free over the water before she'd fallen like a stone into sleep. Mary Margaret had slept that night like she always did. She'd slept like the dead.

Two

BECKY MET HER FATHER AT THE BOTTOM of the stairs. He had his lunch pail in one hand and his keys in the other but when he saw her his face lit up in one of his rare smiles.

"First Monday in June," he said. "I was hoping you'd be down before I left. You all set?"

Becky nodded, hoping he'd notice the new way she'd done her hair, but he was staring over her head now, thinking. "That's good," he said. "That's good. Last night, you know, I was remembering my graduation, what happened then."

"What, Dad?" said Becky, hoping that this time, on this day, he might finally tell her.

"Oh, well," he said. "That was my day. This is

yours. But you might just remind Miss Clough. I don't think it ever happened again, but she's getting old now. I wouldn't want her getting careless with one of mine."

Becky felt a shock run through her. "Miss Clough is never careless," she said.

"I guess not," he said. "And it's been a lot of years, hasn't it? A lot of kids." He looked for a moment as though he might hug her like he used to, but then he just touched her shoulder with his keys. "So don't worry. Just do like Miss Clough says, and concentrate."

"I've been practicing," said Becky. "But it's hard."

"Oh, yeah," he said. "It's hard. But it's worth it. You'll do fine."

In the kitchen, her mother was flipping French toast with one hand and mopping up Billy with the other. He wiggled out from under the washcloth and grinned at Becky, his fists pounding happily on the tray of his highchair.

"Hi, kiddo," said Becky. Her father had dubbed him Billy the Kid about two weeks after he'd come home from the hospital. "Born hell-raiser," he'd said. The pride in his voice, his obvious pride in having fathered an unexpected son, after two daughters, should have made Becky hate the very sight of her little brother. But you couldn't hate Billy.

And Becky didn't. It was just that since he'd been born she wasn't really sure who she *was*. She wasn't the youngest anymore and she wasn't the oldest. She wasn't the only daughter or the only son. Well, that wasn't such a big deal. Lots of people were in the middle. Her mother had been in the middle, actually, and had talked to Becky about how hard it had been growing up between mean Uncle Jim and cute little Aunt Cindy. She understood.

What she didn't understand, because Becky had never tried to tell her, was how Becky felt sometimes that she wasn't anything. Not anything special, anyway. Not very pretty or very smart or very talented. All the other kids in her class shone in something. Penny had personality. Eddy was a genius. Tim was the cutest boy Becky had ever seen. And Mary Margaret? Well, Mary Margaret was a saint, although Becky wasn't quite sure what a saint was and was pretty sure she didn't want to be one herself. But at least it was something. Lots of times lately, Becky just felt like a blob.

Except right at the moment Billy wouldn't let her. He had picked up his syrup-coated car and was holding it out to her proudly. "Ohhhh," she said admiringly. "Billy's car. Billy's bright blue car." She dabbed a finger full of syrup from his tray but shook her head as her mother started to slip a piece of French toast onto her plate.

"I can't," she said. "I'd just throw it back up."

"Oh, Becky," said her mother. She sat down suddenly. "I hate this day. I hated it with Nancy and I hate it with you, and I swear as soon as Billy's old enough to start, he's going over to the elementary school in Alstair if I have to drive him there myself."

Becky shifted uneasily. "It's just that you didn't . . ."

"Yeah," said her mother. She ran both hands through her hair, hard. "I didn't grow up in this town so I don't 'know.' Well, what I do know is that Miss Clough might be a good teacher, but she's not God Almighty."

"Mom, she doesn't think—"

"Yes, she does, sweetie. She does, and so does everybody else in this town, and it gives me the creeps. You know what your father said to me once? This was after all the usual stuff about how smart she was, how she'd read everything, how she knew everything, everything about the natural world and could get even the dumbest kid to understand it because, you don't want to forget, she never gets impatient, she never loses her temper, she—"

"Mom."

"Okay, okay, but what I wanted to tell you was what he said then. He said she could look right into your mind and know what you were thinking. And if she didn't like it, she could change it." She shivered, and Billy started to cry. She lifted him into her lap, but absentmindedly, still talking.

"Change it. Change you. Well, I don't want you changed."

"Mom, that's not what he meant. He—"

"No? Are you going to be the same Becky, *my* Becky, tonight? Are you?" Billy was howling now, and by the time she'd quieted him her voice was quiet again, too.

"I'm sorry. Miss Clough *is* a good teacher and there's no question you all mean the world to her. Like your father says, she's given her life to this town. She *is* this town. So I have to trust her." She leaned over and lifted Becky's face so she could look directly into her eyes. "So good luck and all that, but be careful. And come right home, after. Right after. And wear something warm. It's cold out there, June or no June."

Fifteen minutes later Becky closed the front door behind her and stood looking for a moment at the sugar maples shading the porch. "Chick-a-dee-dee-dee," she called softly. "Chick-a-dee-dee-dee." There was a rustle in the leaves, but the bird that emerged briefly to look at her was a robin.

"Now don't be mad," said Becky. "You were my first choice." *The Secret Garden* was one of Becky's favorite books. Miss Clough had read it to them two years ago, and like Dickon and Mary Lenox, Becky had fallen immediately in love with Ben Weatherstaff's robin. Of course, Miss Clough had explained to them that English robins were different from American ones: smaller and rounder and friendlier. But American robins were special, too, the way they just appeared on the coldest, soggiest day in March, as though of course it was spring and you just hadn't realized it.

"Maybe I'll meet you later today," said Becky, and then swallowed hard. She nodded stiffly as the robin hopped further up into the tree and out of sight. "Maybe I really will."

She walked slowly down the steps. She felt strangely light. No lunch box, no books, nothing to share at recess. She shook her empty arms and then held them out to the sides, feeling the way her shoulders pulled up. What must it feel like to just give a little flick and . . . rise? Rise and glide. Rise and soar into the sky. . . . Chickadees don't soar, she reminded herself. They make short practical flights to places where they can hop around and gather food without wasting too much energy. Or at least that's what her chickadee did.

She knew she should get going. Penny would be wondering where she was, and it would be terrible to be late. But she stood for a last few minutes under the protection of the largest maple and stared at the porch. It sagged a little, and the paint on the ceiling was beginning to peel, and the faded green cushions on the glider were stained with Kool-Aid and Popsicles and the ground-in dirt from bare feet. It was hers, it belonged to the Becky she was now at this very minute. What Becky would look at it tonight? "Are you going to be the same Becky, *my* Becky, tonight? Are you?" Would she?

Suddenly she was running down the driveway and up onto the road. She dodged around the paper box and the battered garbage cans and then crossed to where the sidewalk started on the other side. Mrs. Hagan's lettuce was already up, and her peas; and the rest of the garden, just planted, was staked out in neat rows. Her birdbaths were all scrubbed and full of fresh water, and the feeders were filled not only with seed but with birds. Becky, as she always did, stopped to look.

They were mostly cardinals, of course. Mrs. Hagan was famous for her cardinals. But a few smaller birds, finches, titmice, chickadees, were also trying, mostly unsuccessfully, to elbow their way in. Becky, smiling as she watched, felt her smile fade.

Why hadn't she noticed that before, how small chickadees were? And how big cardinals were, with their strong black beaks, their sharp claws, their confidence. . . . Why, Mrs. Hagan's cardinals could probably run off an eagle if an eagle was dumb enough to come into their yard. What could they do to a chickadee that really got in their way? Where was Mrs. Hagan, anyway? Why wasn't she there, like most mornings, waving or giving a friendly shout about the weather? Why wasn't she there, keeping her cardinals *under control?*

And then Becky realized something else. It wasn't just Mrs. Hagan who was missing. Everybody was missing. It was a Monday morning and the town was empty. No one was out weeding or walking their dog and there was only one pickup parked in front of the hardware. Well, of course, the little kids were all at home and it had been over an hour since the bus had made its pass down the road to take the older ones to Alstair and the junior-senior high school. But why wasn't Miss Stiker out sweeping her front walk or old Mr. Growney hobbling his slow way to the post office like every other morning?

Because it isn't like every other morning. For a moment Becky felt like she'd stepped into a small puddle and gone unexpectedly up to her knees in icy water. The first Monday in June wasn't like any other morning and the whole town knew it. Of course, the post office was closed today. How could she have forgotten that? Everything was closed today except the school and nobody was going to the school except for her and Penny and Eddy and Mary Margaret and Tim.

And Miss Clough. Suddenly Becky could almost see her, Miss Clough: see her long pale face with its beak of nose, her heavy brows over eyes so dark and deep and still that your fear or your anger just sank down into them and disappeared. Are you going home, those eyes seemed to be saying now. Will you go back, where it's safe, where nothing can happen to you? Or will you come to me?

For a long minute Becky stood there, paralyzed. And then she started to run again. She ran past Mr. Henry's beehives and Mrs. Bartz's fishpond and the tree that poor Duane always kept smeared with honey for his ants, and she almost ran right into Mr. Heinman.

Mr. Heinman, an old schoolmate of her father's, was leaning against the open door of his pickup, gazing at the flock of crows perched in raucous chorus on the wires over the hardware store. A cigarette dropped ash from where it hung, forgotten, in his hand and he was smiling faintly as he watched the huge birds. They were as black as the patch over his right eye.

"Morning," he said as Becky stood there, catching her breath, clutching her hands together so they wouldn't tremble, so she wouldn't scream. He took one last drag on his cigarette and ground it under his foot. "I guess I know where you're going in such a hurry."

Do you? thought Becky. Do you? She nodded politely.

"Would you believe it?" he said. "I actually forgot. I drove in here to pick up some roofing nails just like it was any other Monday, and the hardware here's closed tighter than a drum. You know, I wouldn't have thought that I'd ever forget the first Monday in June. Not ever."

"I'd better get going," said Becky. Mr. Heinman

had always made her nervous. Now she almost couldn't stand him. Miss Clough. She needed Miss Clough.

He turned now so that he was staring right at her with his one good eye. "Sure," he said. "And say hello to Miss Clough for me, will you? I always like to be remembered to Miss Clough, and this might be my last chance."

"Last chance?" echoed Becky. She'd never wanted anything more than to get away from Mr. Heinman and his single cold eye, but she was caught by something that hung under his words like the big snapping turtle that lurked, waiting, in the depths of the town-line pond.

"Well, yes," said Mr. Heinman. "This town's been hers for a long time. But not forever."

"I don't know what you mean," said Becky, suddenly not caring if she was rude. "I have to go."

"Yeah, you run along," he said. "You sure don't want to be late to school today. Not today." He clambered into his truck and started it up, sending the crows off, too, screaming into the pale sky.

"Just tell her hello," he said over the roar of his

engine. "And if you think of it, tell her to try a little harder than she did twenty-five years ago, will you?" He adjusted his patch, raised his hand in salute, and, scattering gravel in a fine spray, gunned out onto the road.

Three

"Becky!" Becky turned and saw Penny beckoning to her from the end of her driveway. Relief flooded over her. Penny looked exactly like she always did, and her voice held nothing but its usual impatience with the general slowness of the world. "Come on!"

"I'm coming!" Becky yelled back. She skirted the gas pump in front of the hardware store and walked quickly past the parsonage of the Baptist church, pausing just for a second to smell the last of the lilacs banking Reverend Magner's porch.

Penny grabbed her firmly by the hand. "We don't have time for lilacs. Where have you been? I know, you've been doing something different with your hair, haven't you? I like it. How do I look?" She let go and twirled down the sidewalk and then back again, her hair the perfect look, her mouth the perfect red.

"Great!" said Becky. Penny's dress was the most beautiful flame of color she'd ever seen. But then she shook her head. "But Miss Clough said old clothes, Pen, and I don't think she's going to let you get away with all that lipstick."

"Oh, she's got too many other things to think about today," said Penny. "She won't even notice. You like it? Cherry red. Of course today I'm calling it something different." She grinned at Becky, daring her to ask. Then, before Becky could even open her mouth, she grabbed her hand again and whispered directly into her ear. "Cardinal red."

"Penny!" said Becky and closed her eyes against the immediate and horrible image of a huge bird tearing at her, gouging her. . . . She opened them and it was just Penny, her friend Penny smiling at her, like always. Of course it was. "You're not supposed to tell. It's bad luck."

"That's just silly," said Penny. "Everybody always finds out later, anyway. Where do you think I've been going every day to watch them?"

"Well," said Becky, "Mrs. Hagan's probably." Actually, yesterday she'd seen Penny there, heading around Mrs. Hagan's house to the backyard with its even bigger feeders. Then another awful thought struck her. "You don't know about *me*, do you?"

"Well, I could guess," said Penny. "I saw what kind of seed you bought last week at the feed store, and I know it's something you can watch from your room...." Then she noticed the expression on Becky's face and stopped teasing. "But I don't really know. Not like I know Eddy's got to be some kind of a frog because if it was anything else he'd just die, and I know Tim's something down at the creek because I've seen him there where it crosses under the bridge."

Becky knew Penny wanted her to ask how she'd happened to see Tim under the bridge, but there was something else she wanted to know, something she'd been thinking about for a long time. "Penny," she said, "do you have any idea about Mary Margaret?"

Penny frowned and then shrugged her shoulders. "I don't know," she said almost angrily. "I just don't get Mary Margaret. She's . . ." Then she stopped and shook her head. "You know?"

Becky nodded. She did know. Mary Margaret was so quiet and always seemed so tired, especially in contrast to her hoard of brothers and sisters who burst ahead of her into school every morning. At recess she was always wiping noses and tying shoes, and at lunch Bridget always spilled her milk, or John shoved Joey because he had a bigger apple, or Danny fell off the swing. Mary Margaret's face, always calm, always controlled, just seemed to shrink and fade as the day went on, so that by the time Miss Clough dismissed them all at three you could hardly see it. All you noticed was the hair, those flaming red curls that hung in a babyish tangle past the middle of her back, because her father wouldn't let her get them cut.

"There's Tim," said Penny, her voice brightening. Tim was hunched down on the bottom step of his aunt's porch, and as always when Becky saw him, something inside her seemed to stop working. She could feel herself shrink and freeze, get wooden and prissy, just like all those poor girls in

Gone with the Wind who had to stand there like dummies and watch Scarlett waltz off with all the boys.

Not that Penny was like Scarlett, at least not like Scarlett later in the book when she got so hard and ruthless, but Penny could work the same magic, laugh and tease and toss her head in the right way. Penny could flirt, and Becky had a terrible feeling sometimes that it was something she'd never learn, that it was something you probably couldn't learn if you didn't know how to begin with.

And boys liked it. Even Eddy would get red and grin when Penny teased him, and all he ever did when Becky was around was blink and explain that bullfrogs made the sound they did with some part of them that Becky could never remember the name of. But she didn't mind about Eddy. She'd grown up with Eddy, and she partly felt sorry for him and partly envied him because this thing he had about frogs that made him so weird made him special, too. It made him real somehow. Miss Clough felt the same way, Becky thought. Becky had caught her looking at Eddy sometimes with the same funny mix of pity and pride.

But Eddy wasn't the problem. Tim was the problem, and as Becky watched him get up and slouch toward them she felt her mouth tighten into its usual stiff smile. "Hi, Tim," she said, and watched his eyes sweep past her. He shook his head at Penny's red dress.

"I don't get it," he said. "Is that the kind of thing they bury you in around here?"

Becky couldn't believe she'd heard him right, but Penny just laughed.

"Tim! That's awful. Nobody's burying anybody. This is my graduation dress!"

"Yeah, that's what I mean," said Tim. "I figure we get through this day alive we'll be lucky."

For once Becky forgot about his blond hair and his blue eyes. "What are you talking about?" she said.

"Well," he said, but he looked at her for almost the first time, "what I'm talking about is that this Miss Clough of yours is either some kind of witch or she's nuts. So she either turns us into something and poof! we're gone, or she thinks she's gonna and we end up dead. That's what I'm talking about."

Penny had stopped laughing, and Becky almost

reached over and smacked him in the face. Just wanting to, so unexpectedly and so violently, scared her so much that she grabbed the nearest tree. It was one of the elms that lined the road, and its rough bark dug into her palms. She took a deep breath and looked straight up into the high darkening arch of leaves. Their color was just steadying into the deep green of summer.

"Well, then, you don't have a clue," she said, trying to keep her voice steady. "You haven't even tried to listen to Miss Clough and understand. You think you know everything, don't you? You think you're better than we are, we're just some kind of hicks in the sticks. Well, this isn't the sticks." She knew she was getting louder, but she didn't care. "This is the most special town in the world, because of Miss Clough and what she found out, and she didn't have to share it with everybody but she did and today she's going to share it with us and we're the luckiest—"

She was almost relieved when Tim interrupted, because in two more words she would have started to cry. Tim's face was ugly now and his voice even uglier.

"Lucky! You're all crazy, too. I never saw a town as crazy as this one. All that canned junk I had to eat all winter and now all these gardens full of crappy vegetables, because nobody eats meat, and no hunting or fishing when the creek's full of trout, I've seen them, and no cats even. No cats! My dad would have let me bring my cat, but no, he might kill one of your cute little birdies or cute little mousies and—"

"Shhh!" Penny had forced herself between them, her face bright with excitement. "Shut up, both of you! Miss Clough's coming. She's coming!"

Tim swung to the road side of the elm and leaned straight against it, his arms crossed so tightly that his fingers bent up against his ribs. Becky stared at the ground, smoothing her flannel shirt down and down again. The dirt between the sidewalk and the elm was packed hard and littered with candy wrappers and half-chewed wads of bubble gum, spit out before their time because no gum was allowed in the schoolyard. She hardly saw them. She felt dazed by the anger and the words that had come pouring out of her, and by her hands that still wanted to curl up into fists and hit something as hard as she could hit. And then she felt sick, because the day that was supposed to be so special was already spoiled.

"It's okay," Penny was saying. "I don't think she saw us. It's weird. I've never seen Miss Clough coming to school. She's always just there."

Becky looked up. Penny's words just slid over her, but watching the tall upright figure turn slowly in at the gate, she felt her stomach unclench. She let out a long breath and felt a little better. "What time is it?" she said. "Why isn't the bell ringing?"

Tim's voice came, hoarse and subdued, from the other side of the tree. "Who's going to ring it?" Becky pressed her hands to her head, trying to get it going again. Of course. The fifth graders took turns ringing the bell, and the fifth graders weren't there today. Of course.

"Listen, you guys," said Penny. "It's late. Make up and let's go." She grabbed Becky with one hand and Tim with the other and pushed them onto the sidewalk in front of her. Tim shrugged out of her grip. But then he straightened and jerked his head first toward Becky and then toward the school. His voice was light again, and mocking.

"Yeah, well, if we gotta graduate, we gotta grad-uate. Right?"

Penny nudged Becky encouragingly. "Right, Beck?"

All Becky wanted to do was go home and start the day over again. But she knew her line. "Right," she said.

But as they turned into the schoolyard, she wished she hadn't. Because things weren't right. A bell was ringing now, and it wasn't the old iron bell that hung up over the door, whose dull bong had summoned them to school every day for seven years. It was a hand bell, and Miss Clough was sounding it, raising her hand up and bringing it back down. Five times it rang, and then it stopped.

As the last silvery peal died away, Becky heard one more sound she'd never heard before. It came from the swing. Mary Margaret was swinging up to the elms and down again, over and over again, as high as she could go. Her red hair was streaming out behind her like a flag in a parade, and she was laughing with joy.

Four

"A LIFETIME," SAID MISS CLOUGH. THEY were sitting out behind the school on the bit of level ground that jutted out before beginning a gradual slope toward the creek. The grass was only roughly mown here and only for a space wide enough for two picnic tables and Miss Clough's chair. A few yards away, huge clumps of dandelions mixed with the coarse grass. Farther down they gave way to scrub: sumac, blackberry bushes, chokecherry, a dense protective thicket hiding the creek from sight. Becky could see where the path down started, just behind Miss Clough's chair, but she couldn't see where it ended. She couldn't see the gate.

"A lifetime ago. So long, it hardly seems possible." Miss Clough sighed. "It was a different world then, so different there's no way to make you understand. There was an order to things. There were things to fear, certainly: sickness, failure, death, things you couldn't control. But here, in our part of the world at least, was the feeling that what suffering there was made sense. It fit into a picture you could understand. And at the worst of times, you could always look to the sky and find comfort. There weren't any bombs yet, you see. No bombs. . . ."

A mosquito settled on Becky's arm, and she waved it away. Beside her, Penny was already working systematically at demolishing this week's nail polish, and across from them Tim slouched, his head in one hand, his other picking a long splinter from the table. Eddy was peering at something—a scurry of tiny red spiders from the pines that shaded the tables from the sun, when there was any. Only Mary Margaret sat completely still, her hands folded in front of her and her face, flushed with a faint color, turned unwaveringly toward Miss Clough.

It wasn't what Becky had expected, to be sitting here at the lunch tables behind the school, listening to Miss Clough talk about the past. It wasn't what any of them had expected. Except that it was morning and Miss Clough's words were her own, it could almost be any ordinary day, when for fifteen minutes after they ate, she read them the daily chapter from *Tom Sawyer* or *Treasure Island* or *The Lion, the Witch and the Wardrobe*. But it's not, Becky told herself. This is important. Listen.

"A lifetime ago, I was eighteen years old," said Miss Clough. Becky straightened and Penny looked up. Not *the* past, then. Miss Clough was going to talk about *her* past, something she'd never done before. Never.

"I'd just graduated from normal school, and I decided to take my first teaching job here, because it was 'away,' hours by train from where I'd grown up. Almost 'out west' this was then, if you were a protected young lady from the center of the state, close to a big city. A great adventure.

"I was scared to death, of course. I'd read as much as I could about country schools, and I knew that some of the farm boys would be bigger than I was, and some even older. I knew I'd have to teach five-year-olds and twenty-year-olds, maybe from the same books, and that some days the school would be full and others, when the weather was bad or the farm work was heavy, I'd be pretty much talking to myself. I knew I'd have to keep the school clean and the stove full of wood and supply everything except the most basic books myself. Well, I was ready to try and do all that, if I had to. I just wasn't sure if I could. Because, who was I? I didn't know yet, you see. I didn't know."

Miss Clough stopped for a minute and closed her eyes. Then she pulled herself straighter in her chair and recrossed her ankles. They were the only pretty part of her, Becky and Penny had decided. Everything else about her was shapeless, but her ankles were slim, "elegant," Penny said, and she swore Miss Clough's stockings were the most expensive you could buy and that her shoes must come from the city. Her dresses, now, heaven only knew where she got all those horrible dresses, those dresses that didn't even seem to fit her anymore.

Becky felt rather than heard a movement, and looking up guiltily from Miss Clough's feet, she saw her eyes. They were looking right at Becky, and there was a faint smile on Miss Clough's face. Her mother's voice echoed faintly in Becky's head. "He said she could look right into your mind and know what you were thinking."

And then Becky remembered something else her father had said once. It had been when she was still little. They'd been out for a walk after dinner, and they'd passed by Duane, a man, but a child too, younger than she was, because his brain worked so slowly. They'd waved but hadn't crossed the street to talk to him, because her father said he just wasn't in the mood to listen to an hour's lecture on ants.

"But you know," he'd said, "it isn't just ants that Duane got from Miss Clough. If it wasn't for her, he'd probably have been put in a home somewhere twenty years ago and forgotten. Miss Clough woke him up, got his brain working with those ants, and it's worked well enough since that he's been able to live with his parents, live in the world. Miss Clough wanted something from him, you see, so she got it."

Maybe she wants something from *me*, Becky

thought suddenly, and her face went hot. Miss Clough looked away and continued. Her voice was lower now, quieter, and they all had to strain to hear.

"It was a terrible year. I found I didn't know anything. How to keep order, how to keep the bigger children from bullying the little ones. How to keep the mice out of the chalk cupboard, how to stop Harold Cumming's nose from bleeding every day, how to stop the two Dunleavy girls from wetting their pants all February because it was so cold they wouldn't use the privy. . . ."

They all laughed except for Mary Margaret, who looked like she could imagine it all too well.

"Yes," said Miss Clough. "It's funny now, it's funny even to me, but then it was terrible. Even the few times, the very few times when I could actually teach, when Dwight Collins finally, one day, one minute, understood long division, and the day when I read *The Swiss Family Robinson* all afternoon because everybody begged me not to stop. . . . Those few times were terrible too, because I knew it was what should be happening all the time and wasn't." She was silent again and her gaze was inward. Then she continued.

"So I felt a failure. I felt I'd never be a teacher, and if I weren't a teacher, what would I be? I was plain, you see, tall and plain even then; marriage, children, didn't seem possible. So I felt lost, worse and worse as the spring went on, more and more cut off from everything around me."

"Where did you live?" It was Tim, and they all looked at him in surprise except for Miss Clough, who nodded and answered him, her voice a bit stronger.

"Next door. I had a room with the Reiners, a nice old couple who'd always boarded the school-teacher. They were good people, but very quiet. She did handwork, tatting, you know, and crocheting, and he built models out of matchsticks, great ugly things that took him years. They were good people but not much company." She paused for a moment, but Tim was staring back down at the table.

"So in the evenings, after supper, I walked. I started by walking through town, but there wasn't much town then, and no sidewalk, and the road was always dusty or muddy. It wasn't paved yet. And besides, a single woman walking alone wasn't really proper, and I was the schoolteacher. . . . So one evening I came back to the school, because I'd noticed a cherry tree halfway down the slope to the creek, and I thought I'd like to get down to it and see if it smelled as beautiful as it looked.

"It took me a while to reach it—it was all overgrown and my skirt kept getting caught—but I did, and it did. It smelled as beautiful as it looked, and it just made me feel worse. The natural world, which I'd loved since I was a child and always could count on, couldn't console me this time. Because it wasn't a failure, you see. That tree, just by being there, was doing exactly what it was meant to be doing. That tree just was, connected to the earth and the sky and the insects, to everything. . . ."

Eddy sighed. It was a long deep sigh from the gut, and everybody heard it except him. Penny giggled. "Shhh," said Mary Margaret.

Miss Clough seemed to rouse herself with an effort. Then she smiled. "I know, Eddy," she said.

"Huh?" he said. "What?" Becky looked at him

and then at Penny, and a second later they were laughing so hard and trying not to that they could hardly breathe. Miss Clough leaned back in her chair and waited them out.

"I know this is hard," she said finally, and Becky felt her cheeks flame. Stop acting like a baby, she told herself. Stop it! "Listening is one of the hardest things there is," Miss Clough went on. "But I'm almost done.

"It was that clear time of day, just before dusk, what my father always called 'the hour of the bat.' I couldn't tell if it was bats I was seeing, but something was moving down over the creek below. I felt something stir inside me, as though that movement was tugging at me, pulling me to come and see. I began pushing myself through the bushes, and then, suddenly, I reached a little clearing.

"It was a grassy place, just up from the water, under a giant willow tree. The grass was short there, and very soft, and without even thinking, I sat down. I leaned against the tree and looked out over the water. At that point the creek takes a bend, so even then it was deep there, and slow. And birds were skimming down out of the sky along the water and then up again. Up and down, up and down, as if they were on some kind of giant swing."

"Swallows," whispered Mary Margaret.

"Swallows," said Miss Clough. "And as I watched them, I felt something I'd never felt before. It seemed to come from someplace deep below me, deep in the earth, a low steady vibration, a feeling more than a sound. And the swallows wheeled and darted, wheeled and darted, and I could hardly breathe with the longing, the longing of my whole heart that just for a minute I could be one of them. And then suddenly, just for a minute, I was."

Nobody was restless now. Their eyes were all on her face. It was deathly pale, her own eyes black tunnels under her heavy brows.

"For the briefest instant I was, hanging clear and buoyant, everything around me flashes of dark and light, and then I felt myself dropping, not falling but dropping under my own power, feeling the air under me cool from the water coming up. And then . . .

"And then I was back under the tree, myself

again, but not just myself. Not anymore. Whatever the sound was, the feeling, it was part of me now, I part of it, part of it and a part of everything . . ."

"Crap." Tim's interruption was so sudden, so brutal, that for a moment none of them moved. Then he moved for them all. He swung his legs up and over the picnic bench and stumbled to his feet.

"This is all crap. You can listen to it if you want to. I'm leaving. And it's not because I'm scared, either. That stuff isn't scary. It's just crazy. You're crazy," he said to Miss Clough, and then he turned and ran toward the corner of the school and was gone.

Five

EDDY, HIS FACE CONTORTED IN A WAY Becky had never seen it, started after him. "You creep!" he shouted. "You . . . you . . . turd!" Then he tripped over the vent pipe from the underground oil tank and fell, fell hard, sprawling out flat onto the coarse grass. Slowly he crawled up into a sitting position, his back to them, and cradled his face in his arms. He didn't make a sound, but Becky could tell by the way his shoulders were shaking that he was crying.

"Eddy." Miss Clough's voice was hoarse, but calm. Eddy lifted his head but didn't turn around. "Thank you. That was gallant of you and I appreciate it." Very slowly she pushed herself up from her chair and stood for a moment, looking down the slope toward the creek. "I think we all need a break and something to eat. Penny, could you help me, please? There are drinks inside, and some cookies."

"Oh, yeah, sure," said Penny. She stood up, fingernail polish falling in bright flakes onto the grass, and then bent her head back down to Becky. "Maybe he's still out front," she whispered. "I'll look while I'm inside. Maybe I can talk to him."

"Yeah," said Becky, her eyes on Eddy. "Tell him to go back where he came from. Tell him we don't need him here."

"Becky!" whispered Penny. Her face was half horrified, half pleased. "I thought you liked him."

"You'd better go," said Becky. "Miss Clough is waiting."

"Oh, yeah, sorry Miss Clough," said Penny. "I'm coming. Boy, this is some graduation."

Becky watched them start up the back steps into the school. Miss Clough had motioned Penny to go ahead and waited until the red dress disappeared through the door before beginning the climb herself. Becky wondered if she'd heard what Penny had said about trying to find Tim and talk to him. She wondered, too, how Miss Clough must be feeling about what Tim had said. It was always hard to know what Miss Clough was feeling or thinking. But "crazy." If somebody called me that, thought Becky, I'd be so mad I'd . . . I'd . . . Well, I don't know what I'd do, but I'd get even.

She felt the table shift and turned to see that Mary Margaret was up and was walking over to where Eddy sat, still hunched, by the corner of the school. She pulled a Kleenex from her pocket, dropped it gently on his hands, and sat down on the grass next to him.

It was a familiar scene, and it took Becky a moment to realize why. Joey. Almost every day you could see Mary Margaret and Joey sitting together in just the same way, almost touching, their heads close together. Sometimes they were reading, sometimes talking, but sometimes Mary Margaret was comforting Joey, after their younger brothers had teamed up to tease him or punch him or steal whatever book he'd been reading and toss it over the fence. Mary Margaret would rescue the book, sit down next to Joey, hand him a Kleenex, and talk to him in just the same quiet soothing way she was talking to Eddy now. And just like Joey always did, Eddy now raised his head, picked up the Kleenex, and blew his nose.

Becky felt her own eyes prickle with tears. Some graduation was right. Penny was inside helping Miss Clough, and Mary Margaret was outside helping Eddy. And what was she doing? What good was she? How come she was always on the outside of everything? She swung her legs over the bench and walked over to where Miss Clough's chair stood between two lichen-covered rocks. The path started right behind it and then swerved almost immediately out of sight around a clump of pussy willows. They'd probably been bushes once but had grown into trees, ragged and unimpressive now that their soft flowers had fallen away.

Miss Clough's chair was blocking the way. It was a weathered Adirondack chair with a sloping seat and broad arms. Her old black sweater lay crumpled along the back, and a tall stick Becky had never seen before leaned against one arm. It was brown and gnarled and smooth, with a knob carved out of one end. The knob was covered with designs. No, Becky thought, peering closer. It was letters, in a language she had never seen.

It looked mysterious, magical even, and Becky felt a faint chill thinking about Tim's words earlier that morning. "Some kind of witch or she's nuts. . . . Some kind of witch or she's nuts." Well, Miss Clough wasn't nuts. Becky was sure of that. But a witch? A good witch, of course, but still . . .

Suddenly, tired of words and thoughts and all the confusing emotions of the morning, Becky squeezed by the chair and stood at the top of the path. A breeze came up from the creek below, and then a familiar sound.

Chick-a-dee-dee-dee. Chick-a-dee-dee-dee. A small black-capped bird was perched along a branch of the willow, its bright eyes turned right toward her. Just like Ben Weatherstaff's robin, thought Becky, her heart lightening, and like Mary Lenox, she answered.

"Chick-a-dee-dee-dee. Chick-a-dee-dee-dee." Oh, I wish I could follow you, she thought, like Mary followed the robin and discovered the key to the garden. Right now. I wish I could follow you all by myself right this minute, down the path and through the gate . . .

"Becky?" It was Eddy. He was limping toward her. His face was streaked and there was a scrape on one cheek, making him look older, almost tough. There was even a new urgency in his voice. "You're not going down there, are you? Not before Miss Clough . . . ?"

"You scared away my chickadee," Becky said. Then she sighed. "I guess not. Eddy, did you ever go down there? By yourself?"

He plopped down into the chair and looked at his hands. They were scraped, too, and grass-stained. "We're not supposed to," he said, sounding like himself again. "Nobody's supposed to, not until graduation."

"I know we're not supposed to, but did you?"

"*I* did." Becky and Eddy both looked up in surprise. Mary Margaret had come silently across the grass, and now she sat down in front of the chair and picked up Miss Clough's stick. "I did once, last fall. It was just before Colleen was born, Columbus Day, and Dad took all the kids to the Harvest Festival to let Mom get some rest but I said I didn't feel well, so Dad let me stay home, too." She ran her fingers over the mysterious letters.

"I lied. I felt okay. I just wanted to be home by myself, with just Mom. I thought . . . Well, it doesn't matter. Mom really did feel crummy. She really did need to rest. So while she was asleep, I came here to the school. I thought maybe I'd get a book to read, but it was locked. I didn't know that, that Miss Clough locked the school when we're not here."

"There's valuable stuff in there," said Eddy gruffly. "The microscope and her collections and a lot of the books. They're all hers, she buys them, not the school."

"I guess so," said Mary Margaret. "But, I don't know, I felt mad at her. I thought it was going to be such a nice day, and it wasn't. It was my fault because I'd lied. I'd sinned."

Becky stirred uneasily and looked away. Mary Margaret sounded funny, talking about sin in such a calm, quiet voice. It was almost a smiling voice, but the kind of smile that had something under it, something Becky didn't want to see. And she hated it when people talked about sin and hell and things like that. It was probably because her family didn't go to church much so she wasn't used to it. But she hated it.

Mary Margaret's even words continued. "And you know it's true, when you sin you want to sin more. Like getting mad at Miss Clough for no reason at all, so then I just wanted something worse. I wanted to do something really bad, as bad as I felt. So I came here behind the school and I went down the path."

Eddy struggled up from the chair. "I shouldn't be sitting here," he said. "You'd better get back, Becky. Back on this side."

But Becky was already coming. She'd felt all at once that the path was going to start tugging her, pulling her as it had pulled Miss Clough so long ago. Down it would pull her, down to something terrifying.

"See?" said Mary Margaret, as, a little breathless, they plopped down onto the grass beside her. The smile had come out of her voice now and was playing around her mouth. "You even feel it, how bad I was."

Suddenly Becky wanted to shake her. "But

what happened?" she said impatiently. "When you went down. Did anything happen?"

Mary Margaret hesitated, and then her face closed down as though she'd thrown a switch. She stood up and propped the stick back against Miss Clough's chair. "Nothing happened," she said. "It's just a path with a gate at the bottom. The gate was locked. There's Penny. She probably needs some help."

Penny was waving from the top of the stairs but not to Mary Margaret. "Becky!" she called. "Come here! Miss Clough wants you."

She saw me, thought Becky immediately. She saw me where I wasn't supposed to be, and now she's going to tell me if I can't obey the rules I can just go home. No graduation for Becky. She could see from the look on Eddy's face that he was thinking the same thing. "Oh, please," she whispered. She got up, smoothed down her hair, and took a big breath. "Please."

But when she walked into the dim coolness of the schoolroom, she could tell immediately that Miss Clough wasn't angry. The teacher was sitting at her desk, a half-empty glass of water on the blotter in front of her. She looked smaller, slumped, but when she saw Becky she straightened and gave her usual calm nod.

"Eddy's all right," she said, more a statement than a question, and Becky nodded.

"Just a little scraped. Mary Margaret helped him."

"Mary Margaret," repeated Miss Clough. She shook her head impatiently and then straightened even further and motioned Becky to her.

"It's important that Tim come back," she said. "I need you to find him and talk to him. He's probably gone to the bridge."

Without thinking, Becky sat down at her desk. It was the second desk in the middle row, the row where the sixth graders always sat, dividing the little kids from the fourth and fifth graders. Two years ago Nancy had sat at this desk, and twenty-five years ago, so had their father. There was hardly an inch on it that hadn't been claimed and branded by somebody Becky had known all her life. She'd carved her own name as close to her father's as she could, and her fingers now traced the worn grooves of the letters he'd made so long ago. W I L L.

"Did you ever have anybody else like Tim?" she asked. "Anybody new?"

Miss Clough was silent for a moment and then nodded. "Oh, yes," she said. "Families have moved here over the years, attracted by country and clean air and . . . things they may have heard. But not very many. The town is dying, you know. It's getting too expensive to farm, and we're just too far from the city to make working there easy, even though I know people do it. Your father, for instance." Becky nodded.

"New children," Miss Clough went on slowly. "Yes, there have been some. But people with children usually move in the summer. They know how hard it is to come into a new school partway through the year. And always, the children have been younger. The oldest new one I had was Suzy Kerr, Susan Hagan now, Mrs. Hagan. She came when she was ten, just starting fifth grade. And it was hard for her. She was a city girl, born and bred in Miami." Her eyes gleamed a little, amused, remembering.

"Miami," said Becky softly. She could almost

see Mrs. Hagan, a little Mrs. Hagan, in a bright red bathing suit, digging in white sand under a palm tree in Florida. And then coming here. "But she was okay, wasn't she? She graduated? She stayed here?"

"She was okay," agreed Miss Clough slowly. "But Tim . . . I think if Tim fails to graduate . . . it will not be okay. For him, especially, but for all the rest of us as well."

Becky swallowed and stood up. "I'll try," she said. "But Miss Clough? Penny might be better. He . . . he likes Penny."

"Yes," said Miss Clough. "But he'll listen to you." Again, Becky felt herself drawn into Miss Clough's gaze and then, with a jolt, let go. A look of great weariness came into Miss Clough's face. "Try and find him, Becky. As quickly as you can."

Becky started for the door and then, with a spurt of new-found courage, turned with one more question. "Miss Clough, if I find him, would you tell me what happened twenty-five years ago? When my father graduated? When Mr. Heinman did?"

"Twenty-five years ago." Miss Clough pushed her hands against her desk and carefully stood up. "Oh, yes," she said, and there was a note of sadness in her voice that Becky had never heard before. "I'll tell you. I'll tell you all."

Six

But Tim wasn't at the bridge. He was sitting in the farthest corner of the boys' side of the schoolyard in the hidey-hole formed by a mass of forsythia bushes. The small clearing had always served as a safe place where by unspoken agreement somebody who wanted to be alone for a while would be left alone. The girls had a similar spot behind the small shed that housed the lawn mower, rakes, and snow shovels. They were places where you could crawl away and hunch down and nobody could see you cry.

Becky wouldn't have seen Tim now if he hadn't moved. Almost at the fence, she heard the bushes rustle and, turning, saw a blue shirt surface and then disappear. "Tim?" she called. There was no answer.

Becky hesitated. Miss Clough wanted her to find Tim, and she'd found him. But he wasn't only on the boys' side, where girls never went, but in a place where he was supposed to be left alone. Finally, she went through the fence and walked slowly down the outside. The road was still quiet, the sidewalk still empty as far as she could see. Checking first for dog droppings, she squatted down, her back to the chain links. Her heart was thudding, and she had to swallow three times before she could work up the saliva to speak.

"Tim?" she said again, softly. "Tim, we . . . we can't graduate without you."

"You think I care? Leave me alone." His voice was right behind her and Becky winced as though she'd been hit.

"I . . . can't. Tim, it's your graduation, too."

"Didn't you hear what I said back there? It's crap. All of it's crap."

Becky struggled to find something that would make him listen. "What's your cat's name?" she said.

"What?"

"Your cat. You said you had a cat."

"Oh, yeah. I *had* a cat. I *had* a lot of things." The bushes thrashed furiously. Becky waited.

"Boone," he said finally. "He was striped, like this hat Daniel Boone wore in a book I read once. He was a big old guy. He couldn't come here, and Dad couldn't keep him, so you know where he took him? He took him to the pound."

"Oh, Tim," said Becky. She realized her eyes were wet, and she sniffed hard, trying to keep the tears back, trying to stay calm and say the right thing, even though she didn't have any idea at all what the right thing was.

Suddenly a finger dug into her back. "What are *you* crying about?" he said, his voice now right in her ear.

"Because you could have had him here. We had a cat once, her name was Snow, but then my sister Nancy got allergic and we had to give him away. Lots of people have cats. They just keep them inside, except on the farms or at the feed store where they have to let them hunt."

"Why can't they all hunt?" His voice was

hoarse. "Cats, they're supposed to hunt. And people too. How do you think all those Indians kept alive if they didn't hunt and fish?"

"I know," said Becky, struggling to get it clear in her own mind, make it clear to him. "I know. But it isn't that hunting's bad, if you have to, to live. And even meat, eating meat, you were wrong about that. People *do* here, especially farm people, animals they raise, that's part of their lives, that's different. It's when you do it for fun, hunt, kill, for *fun*. That's what cats do, if you let them, even if you feed them. You say 'supposed to,' okay, but . . ."

Then she turned, grabbed the fence with both hands and shook it. "But what if every time a cat was ripping into a bird it was ripping into you? What if every time it grabbed a mouse and shook it and tortured it, you could *feel* it, not just feel sad for it or sorry for it, but *feel* it, the terror and the pain, feel it through every part of you? Don't you see? That's what graduation does. Because once you are a bird or a mouse or a snake or a spider, even for a minute, then you know.

"And don't call it crap or crazy. It isn't. My father's not crazy and he knows. So does my sister and Penny's mom and everybody who's graduated here for years and years. And if I don't know, if I don't get to know . . ." Through the fence she was glaring into his face and crying hard now, and she didn't care.

He slammed his hand against the fence, making the chain links rattle. "But I don't get it. Who'd want that? If it's so awful, I mean, if every time you stepped on an ant you felt, you felt . . . like that. Then who'd want to know?"

Becky rubbed her arm across her face, but it was a minute before she could speak. "Because that's only part of it. Haven't you been listening to Miss Clough at all? You get everything. You can see things and hear things and smell things, all the things people have forgotten, you get to remember. You can feel how it is to . . . to swim in under the bank of the creek and hang there in the current, or burrow down under a grassy meadow that goes on forever." She shivered. "You can feel how it is to fly!"

Now he was staring as fiercely at her as she had at him, his dark blue eyes almost as black as Miss Clough's.

"You really believe that."

"I know it," she said.

He chewed his lip. "Your father?" he said.

She nodded. "And my grandfather. When he'd walk in the back pasture, snakes would come right up out of the creek and curl around his feet."

His eyes narrowed. "But snakes . . . snakes hunt. So then you'd feel . . . that, too?"

Becky nodded.

"Wow," he said. "Wow."

"Yeah," she said, and shuddered. "It's awful. It's scary. But that's why we need everybody. That's why we need you."

He nodded slowly. "But maybe I still can't do it," he said. "Maybe I still won't want to."

"I don't know," said Becky. "But Miss Clough will. As long as you come. As long as you're there."

"Yeah," he said. "Yeah." He stood up and Becky did, too. "Yeah," he said once more and wiped his hands down hard over his face. He looked at Becky out of the corner of his eye and then nodded abruptly. "Okay," he said and immediately disappeared back into the bushes.

Becky took a deep breath and let it out. She'd done it. She'd actually done it. And now, they'd go back together and everybody would see that . . . well . . . she and Tim were . . . well, friends.

But by the time she'd come through the fence again into the playground Tim was almost out of sight. Running, she caught up with him just as his long stride turned to a saunter. He ignored her, slouched over to the picnic table, and grabbed a cookie. Glancing at Miss Clough, he muttered something, stuffed the cookie into his mouth, and threw himself down on the grass.

Miss Clough nodded at him, not even seeming to notice that Becky was back, too, that Becky had done the job she'd been sent to do. Becky, hating herself, felt her eyes fill again and almost overflow. She blinked hard, tilting her chin so that no stupid telltale tear could trickle up and over and give her away. Then she walked carefully over to the table, swung onto the bench next to Penny, and reached for the plate.

"Where have *you* been?" said Penny. Her eyes were hard. " 'Tell him to go back where he came from,' " she mimicked in a shrill whisper. " 'Tell him we don't need him here.' That's what you *said*."

For a moment Becky saw her as she had earlier, all black beak, sharp claws, wings red as blood. She shrank away, and the image faded. "Penny, Miss Clough asked me. He . . ." She saw again the humiliating sight of Tim hurrying away from her. "He's a jerk," she whispered, almost spitting it out and wishing it was true.

"Well, okay then," said Penny, but her expression was still cool. "Your face is all blotchy," she said and then turned away to whisper something to Eddy, who was glowering at the back of Tim's head.

"It's time," said Miss Clough. "Past time. We need to move down to the creek. If the girls would take the refreshments back into the school, I'd appreciate it if the boys would move my chair."

"I can do it myself, Miss Clough," said Eddy, almost falling as he clambered over the bench.

"I'm sure you can, Eddy," said Miss Clough. "But it's a heavy chair and I'd prefer that you both do it. However, Eddy, you can give me a hand getting up and then give me my stick. And Tim, when we start, I'd like you to carry this basket. It's sandwiches, for after. You'll all be hungry then."

Becky blindly picked up her glass and drained it. But even Kool-Aid couldn't dissolve the feeling that was growing in her like a lump of raw dough. Rising, she took the pitcher, slipped by Penny and went slowly up the stairs to where Mary Margaret was standing with a loaded tray. She opened the door for them both. Penny hadn't moved except to idly brush crumbs off the table. She was watching the boys, both scowling, as they wrestled the big chair up and away from the path.

Becky shut the door hard behind her. "Mary Margaret," she said. "Is this the way you thought it would be?"

Mary Margaret stood very still and then turned and looked at Becky. Her eyes were gray, flecked with green, and they looked enormous in her pale face. "It doesn't matter," she said.

Becky forced her voice to remain calm, even though she could feel the lump inside her expand. First Tim and Miss Clough, then Penny, and now Mary Margaret. It was as if they were all behind some kind of tall fence and she was still outside and they hadn't even noticed. "Well, it matters to me," she said.

"I mean it doesn't matter about *here*," said Mary Margaret. "When we get down there, after we go through the gate, it will be okay. You'll see."

"Will it?" said Becky. She looked at Miss Clough's desk and for a minute saw not Miss Clough but an old, sick, very tired woman, a woman tired almost to death.

Mary Margaret's gaze followed Becky's, and then she smiled her funny little smile. "She doesn't matter either," she said softly. "Not when we get down there, down there on the other side of the gate."

Becky shivered, and suddenly the lump of hurt and humiliation collapsed under something cold and certain and clear as ice. "You've been there, haven't you?" she said. "That time, last fall. You didn't just go down the path. You went through the gate."

"Oh, no," said Mary Margaret. She shook her head and kept shaking it, as though rubbing something out that she didn't want Becky to see. "I couldn't go through it. It was locked."

"You're lying," said Becky.

"Oh, no," repeated Mary Margaret. "I wouldn't lie to you about something like that, Becky. That would be a sin."

Becky stared at her, at her calm eyes and her calm little smile, and then shook her head. "Maybe you're not lying. But you're not telling the truth, either." She straightened her shoulders and took a deep breath. Yes. The lump was gone.

Mary Margaret wasn't telling the truth about the gate and she wasn't telling the truth about Miss Clough, either. "I don't think you know what's true and what's a lie," Becky went on. "But Miss Clough does. And Miss Clough matters, too. It will be okay. Because Miss Clough will make it be."

And miraculously, when a few minutes later they all started down the path behind Miss Clough, she did. She led the way slowly but firmly, her stick sounding a solid processional note against the packed rocky soil underfoot. All around them was green, a warm green, even under the cool gray sky. It smelled of clover. Butterflies flitted among the tall grass, and bees hummed so close in the honey-suckles that bordered part of the path that they all instinctively slowed and moved closer together.

They passed under a tree, a gnarled old cherry, to which a few lingering blossoms still clung, its scent a faint echo of past glory. Becky reached out a finger and touched it. She had pushed Mary Margaret out of her mind. She had pushed everything out of her mind and felt free, as though she floated, buoyant, in a timeless stream.

The path curved and narrowed. It was spongier underfoot now, and the honeysuckle had given way to tall plumey marsh grass and cattails and sumac. A red-winged blackbird flew up from nowhere and perched, swinging, from a clump of loosestrife. The only sound now came from their footsteps and the bubble of water moving near them, over stones.

And then the path made one last bend, and in front of them was the gate.

Seven

IT WAS, BECKY SAW IMMEDIATELY, NOT A
serious gate. That is, it wasn't attached to a fence,
so that anybody could squeeze around it if they really wanted to and didn't mind getting their feet
wet. She glanced back at Mary Margaret and then
away. She still didn't want to think about Mary
Margaret and what she might have done. But it
was hard not to, because it was clear that the gate,
the famous gate, wasn't built to keep out anybody
who was determined to get to the other side.

Even so, it was beautiful. It was made of some
kind of metal that glowed like polished old pen-
nies. The metal had been turned and curved into a
flowing design that radiated out from the central

figure of a willow tree drooping over a pool. Small animals and reptiles sheltered beneath it; the sky above was bright with birds. Becky noticed an intricately molded spider's web weed-caught above the fish-filled pool. Butterflies and insects gleamed from every corner, and Eddy, squatting down, put his finger awkwardly on a small frog poised to leap at a glistening fly.

But it was more than beautiful. As Miss Clough inserted and turned the heavy key, Becky could feel the gate's power. She moved toward it and then through it with no conscious thought, and one by one the others followed. They all walked silently and carefully, as though carrying something precious and breakable from a safe familiar world to one unknown, perhaps dangerous.

Becky turned and watched them come. Tim was chewing on his lower lip. Eddy was blinking hard, and the red of Penny's lipstick stood out from her bleached face like a stop sign against snow. Mary Margaret, always pale, looked ready to faint. But she steadied herself, and at a nod from Miss Clough, closed the gate behind her. Becky, her own heart finally slowing, saw her shut her eyes and whisper something. A prayer? A spell? Becky shivered and looked away.

The path now turned sharply to the right and up, and Miss Clough, leaning heavily on her stick, motioned them on ahead. As they climbed, the ground to their left dropped, forming a steep bank of rocks and eroded tree roots and opening a view to the water below. As Miss Clough had said, the creek curved here, slowed, and deepened to form a pool. Behind her, Becky heard a sharp intake of breath. It was Tim, and they all turned and followed his gaze to a mossy log that stuck out over the water. As they watched, something uncurled from it and dropped down and was gone.

Penny shuddered. "A snake," she said. "There aren't any more, are there? Up here?"

"I doubt it. That was a water snake and water is where they like to be." Miss Clough had caught up with them and was breathing heavily, sweat trickling down her face. She looked fixedly at the empty log for a moment and then shook her head. "No snakes," she said and then pointed up the path with her stick. "Just a little farther now, around that clump of poplars."

A scent that had been hanging in the background intensified now into a heavy sweetness, and as Becky led the way the last few feet, she wasn't surprised to see, banked behind a clearing of soft grass, a deep row of lilacs. They were old trees that had survived by reaching up and toward the sun and they were heavy with clusters of dark purple just past their prime. She stood, her eyes closed, breathing in the overwhelming smell of early summer. Then, just for a moment, she felt dizzy, as though the earth, deep under her feet, had shifted. She shook her head to clear it, and when she opened her eyes, Miss Clough was beside her. "But where's the willow?" she found herself saying.

"It came down long ago," said Miss Clough. She was leaning hard on her stick, her breath slowly quieting. "Willows are fragile. It was fairly sheltered here, but about thirty-five years ago we had a storm that took most of the trees along the creek. I was heartbroken at first, but I'd already planted one lilac here and could see that more would be useful. So I never replaced the willow." She walked slowly to a bench set under the largest poplar and carefully lowered herself down. Tim set the basket beside her.

"What do you mean, useful, Miss Clough?" said Penny as they all settled themselves on the ground. Penny seemed to have forgiven Becky for whatever she thought Becky might have done and was sitting close enough to her that their shoulders touched. It felt good, that familiar friendly touch, and Becky relaxed, running her fingers over the grass. She had never felt grass like it. It was heavy, springy, and dark green, a living carpet fed by black earth and deep cold water, and was so thick that no weeds had been able to penetrate its mass of deeply seated roots. It felt so alive that Becky could almost hear it. What was it that people said? Humming with life? . . . It was humming with life.

"Smell," said Miss Clough. "All of you, close your eyes and breathe in as fully as you can. Soak yourself in it. This is lilac, as only you can perceive it. This is lilac chosen by a human mind, planted by human hands. It will bring you back."

A chill ran through Becky, and opening her eyes she saw that Mary Margaret's hands were clenched so tightly around her knees that her knuckles showed like bone. Tim's hands, too, were clenched, but deep into the grass, as though holding for dear life onto the earth below. They're scared too, thought Becky. They're even more scared than me.

"*One* of the things that will bring you back," Miss Clough went on quietly. "Another is time. You've all been practicing, I hope, and you'll be setting the clock inside your head to three. A third is the thing you've left with me. If you remember, I asked you all weeks ago to bring me something small that was important to you, something that meant family to you, or friendship. Something that made you laugh or cry, expressions of emotion only we, as humans, can use." She touched the basket beside her. "I have them all here."

"Couldn't you go with us, Miss Clough?" Becky saw Penny nod at Eddy's blurted words. She knew how they felt, too. It would be so comforting to know that Miss Clough was there, even if you couldn't recognize her or hear her or touch her. But she also knew what Miss Clough's answer would be.

"I need to stay here. Someone must always stay, because if all else fails, it's what's here that brings you back. And I'm here. Remember that. I'm here and I will always bring you back." Miss Clough looked at them each in turn and then repeated her promise almost in a whisper. "I will always bring you back."

They all let out their breaths as though that was what they were waiting to hear, and Becky, sitting right next to Miss Clough's bench, was the only one who heard her brief gasp, immediately muted. For a moment Miss Clough looked carved from stone, and her hand tightened on the knob of her stick until it seemed part of it. Then she relaxed, but her face now was clammy and gray, and her eyes had sunk so deeply into their sockets that Becky could see nothing but a dull black gleam.

"Miss Clough?" she whispered. "Miss Clough?"

Slowly the teacher turned her head. For a moment her eyes stayed dead. Then she lifted her chin and was herself again, although her voice was a little dazed. "Yes, Becky?"

"I'm sorry," said Becky and then thought of what she could say. "I'm sorry, but you said that you'd tell me, tell us, about that other graduation. The one twenty-five years ago."

"Yes," said Miss Clough. "Yes." It seemed to take her a moment to remember. "That was the time your father graduated, wasn't it? And Mary Gillian. And Joe Burnie." She was silent. "And of course Peter Heinman . . ."

Becky nodded. "I saw Mr. Heinman this morning, and he said to say hello." She swallowed. "He said he always liked to be remembered to you on the first Monday in June."

"I'm sure he does," said Miss Clough. "I'm sure he does." She let her breath out slowly. "And he's right. It's very important to remember that graduation. It's important that every sixth-grade class knows what can happen. What did happen." Then she leaned forward, her voice stronger.

"First, though, you must separate Mr. Heinman, the adult you know now, from the twelve-year-old boy who was Peter Heinman twenty-five years ago. Mr. Heinman now is a private man with a private life you must all respect. After you hear this story, you must think no less of him. In fact, you must think more of him, as a man who allows you, as an aid to you, to invade his privacy by hearing about a terrible time in his life. Do you understand?"

They all nodded. Penny's eyes were very wide, and Eddy hunched closer. Mary Margaret's hands were clasped tightly in her lap. Only Tim shifted and turned partly away as if he didn't want to hear what Miss Clough was going to say.

"I never had a boy who hated school more," said Miss Clough. "He hated everything about it: the books and the homework and the tests. Well, that's natural enough, everybody hates all of that a lot of the time. But Peter hated everything. He hated art. He hated music and spelling bees. He even hated parties. You see, what he really hated was the whole idea of being shut up in a room with a lot of other people." Miss Clough shook her head.

"They say teachers can change children. Mold them. Well, maybe a little, if a child wants to change, sees something better in it. But Peter Heinman didn't want to. He was a boy who knew exactly who he was and liked exactly how he locked into his world."

"But maybe he didn't." It was Mary Margaret, who had edged closer, the words seeming to blurt out of her unbidden. She was trembling. "But maybe the way things were, there wasn't any point, any point in wanting something different. Maybe he wanted to change things more than anything in the world, but he couldn't. . . ." She fumbled to a stop.

"I don't think so," said Miss Clough, but she gave Mary Margaret a brief glance of interest before going on. "No," she said to them all, "if you want to badly enough, you can always change things. That's what hope is, why there's always a point to hope. But hope takes courage. It's easy to shut down, shut hope out, give it up. Give it up to self-hatred, to despair. But giving up hope is the worst thing there is. Isn't that right?"

Mary Margaret was sitting rigidly, gazing down at the ground. She shook her head. "I don't know," she whispered. "I don't know." But Miss Clough didn't seem to hear her. She was looking at Tim, her gaze intent on his averted face. She waited a long minute and then spoke again, faster now, as though eager to finish.

"I don't think Peter Heinman knew anything about despair. He knew he was a person who needed to be alone. Alone and outside and walking the fields of his father's farm. He wanted to farm and he knew how to farm and everything else was useless to him. Useless."

She shook her head again. "I shouldn't have forced him to graduate. But I thought it might be . . . the one thing I could give him that would have some meaning for him. I should have known how wrong I was when he said two things. He said first that he was only doing it because his father would whip him if he didn't, if he flunked and got left behind. I never knew Peter's father, he'd left school before I came, so it wasn't that he believed in graduation, or at least in a graduation that could give someone more than a piece of paper to hang on the wall. But he believed in rules and in Peter following them. Peter would do what he was told. That was that.

"The second thing Peter said was that if he had to pick something he'd pick a crow, because the better he could understand what went on in a crow's head the better he'd know how to get rid of them when they came to steal his corn. But I could tell he didn't believe it, didn't believe it would really happen. His father didn't, you see. So why should he?

"It's always dangerous if you don't believe in graduation. Too much of you stays human, not just the little bit that lets most of us experience what we experience and then lets us come back and remember it. And if you couple not believing with hating what it is you've chosen . . ."

Miss Clough grasped her stick with both hands, as though seeking strength for what she finally had to say.

"Peter Heinman's bad luck was that it did happen, and that he got in with a flock of crows. They attacked him immediately and mauled him so badly that he spent most of the summer in the hospital, recovering. But the one thing he never recovered was the use of his right eye. They'd pecked it out."

Eight

It was Tim who broke the silence. His voice was hoarse. "That could happen to me, couldn't it?"

"It could," said Miss Clough. "That's why I'm not forcing you to try."

"But you're letting me."

"Letting you," she repeated. "Yes, that's part of graduation, too. Making that choice."

Suddenly he pounded the ground with his fist. "How can I . . . You're saying it's like *Peter Pan?*"

Miss Clough looked puzzled.

Becky understood. She'd seen the movie version three times. "Tinker Bell," she said to Miss

Clough. "You know. If you don't believe in Tinker Bell, she stops glowing. She . . . dies."

"I see," said Miss Clough. "Yes, I remember now. It's been a long time since I've read Barrie. I never did much like *Peter Pan,* all those boys who didn't want to grow up. But yes, I guess it is something like that." She leaned toward Tim. "And the thing is, you must not only *want* to believe, you must *need* to. That need might be forced on you from the outside, as his father and I forced it on Peter Heinman. But it only really works if it comes from within. I mean, works as a blessing and not as a curse. So can you do that? Can you need to, enough?"

Tim was chewing his bottom lip again. "I don't know," he said. Then he caught Becky's eye. He held it for a second and then looked at Penny beside her. Then his head came up and he ran a hand over his short blond hair. "Sure," he said, shrugging for a second back into his old role. "Why not?"

"Miss Clough?" said Becky. She suddenly felt afraid. But Miss Clough ignored her.

"Good," she said to Tim. "Then it's time. But just one more thing. For all of you. You must all remember that even if you do believe strongly, when you become what you have chosen, the part of you that stays human is a danger to you. It sets you apart, and the others will sense it. Almost always they'll just shun you, because you'll frighten them. But once in a while they'll attack, especially a male who feels his territory or his mate are being threatened. And of course, there are always predators. For one of you this is a special danger but I've already talked to that person about avoiding certain places, taking extra care. All in all, don't try and get too close to other creatures. You'll feel kinship enough without getting too close. Do you understand?"

Understand? Becky felt that she understood nothing except that fear was flooding her now almost to the panic point. She looked wildly at the others. Penny and Eddy were nodding, Tim shrugging impatiently. Mary Margaret . . . Becky willed herself calm, willed herself to study the strange look on Mary Margaret's face. Because it was strange. Why? She'd seen it before, that look. Where? *Where?* In the city. Yes. Once in a city museum Becky had seen someone with the look Mary Margaret had now.

She strained to remember. It had been the picture of someone being burned alive, looking upward at a bird the guide told them was really his soul flying toward heaven. His face had been full of awful pain, but happy, too, and it had made Becky feel sick. And she felt sick now. She felt afraid again, not panicky anymore but with a cold certain feeling that something was very wrong.

Should she tell Miss Clough? But Miss Clough hadn't wanted to hear about Tim. And besides, what could she say? "Mary Margaret looks funny? Looks . . . scary? And maybe she's been here before? Done this before?" They would all think she was crazy. No, she had to trust Miss Clough. She just had to.

Miss Clough was speaking again now, speaking slowly, as if every word was suddenly an effort. "All right," she said. "Now, I want everyone to stand up and stretch. Stretch hard up, then down. Then shake yourself out. You want to be as loose and flexible as possible. And don't watch anyone else. Concentrate on yourself, your body, how the muscles feel, how it feels to be you."

Becky kept her eyes on the ground. Concentrate on yourself, she thought. Not Mary Margaret. Not Tim. Yourself. She felt the pull of her muscles, the stretch of her spine. Her heart was drumming in her ears, and she could feel sweat forming on her upper lip. It was noon now, a bit warmer, and very still. It felt like something waiting to happen.

"Now," said Miss Clough. "Spread out and then go and sit facing the creek. Cross your legs, put your hands in your lap and sit up as straight as you can." Becky, passing by Penny, saw that she was shaking. "Oh, Becky," she heard her whisper. "I'm scared. I'm just so scared."

"You'll be fine, Penny," said Miss Clough. She was standing now behind them. Her voice was low, and her words were slow and calm, calm and relaxed, relaxed and confident. "You'll all be fine." All fine, thought Becky. All fine. Miss Clough knows. Now pay attention. Pay attention.

"Close your eyes," said Miss Clough. "Now, set your clock. Set it for three. See the numbers of the clock set at three and then draw it back, back and down, deep down inside your head. You will return at three. You will return at three."

I will return at three, thought Becky. At three.

And now I will settle. I will settle down into it. I will settle down into the silence, into the hum, into the power of the day and the place, my need and my belief.

And starting at my head I will move down, too, down through myself, giving myself up. Hair and skin to feathers. Mouth to beak. Arms to wings. Smaller and smaller. Legs shrink, scales form, feet to claws. Down and down. Deeper and deeper. Me at the core. Me at the core. Not afraid anymore, but changed. Changed for now. Changed, a part of me, for always.

And suddenly she was no longer moving down but up. Air moved past her, she was part of the air, she was moving the air. She was beating against it, then catching it or being caught by it, and then again, beating into it, up and up. It was a game, a wonderful game, played with everything she had, everything she was. It was played against no one else, for no one else; it was played for no reason except joy, the sheer joy of it.

Then, high enough, tiring, she reached out, grabbed—her perch rough, familiar, swaying but secure. Everything around her now was flickering light and she was part of the light, part of the leafy shelter rising above her and around her. Safe. But more than safe. Clinging there, she felt absolutely real, absolutely right, just as she was at this very moment. There was nothing more beautiful, more alive than she was, high up and rocking, rocking into shade and then back into light. Something moved up from deep inside her and broke irresistibly into sound.

Chick-a-dee-dee-dee. Chick-a-dee-dee-dee.

ꟸ   ꟸ   ꟸ

Eddy was seated on the grass in front of Miss Clough. Tears were running down his face and he was looking up to where birdsong was echoing again and again from the poplar above him. "I can't make it work. I'll never make it work, never change, never be what I'm supposed to be. Never!"

"It's all right, Eddy," said Miss Clough. "You're feeling now, you've forgotten your facts, you're on your way. You're feeling. Now concentrate. What do you hear? What do you smell and see? Get inside it, give yourself up to it. You know it, you feel it, now become it. Become it, Eddy."

Eddy hunched around himself, his head deep in his arms, sweat dripping down his neck onto the grass. And then something clicked in his brain. He could feel it, feel something close, something open. He hunched deeper and deeper through the opening, smaller and smaller, and then, suddenly, he was gone.

Everything was sensation. For a long moment he drowned in it, it was too much. He was overwhelmed by sheer sight, sheer touch, sheer *sense*, except that it made no sense. He was listening with his skin, seeing with his tongue, feeling with every inch of him because every inch of him was open and he couldn't shut it down, couldn't shut it off. He couldn't escape.

And then, all at once, trying to escape, he didn't want to anymore. He didn't need to. He jumped, and as he always thought about it later, it was funny, the sound of it, but right, right: he jumped into his own skin. All that sensation, all that feeling, *fit*. It fit him, he could claim it now. He didn't have to fight it anymore or be afraid of it. And he never would have to again.

Maybe he wouldn't be perfect, nothing was perfect. But what he was wasn't a tadpole anymore. He had legs now, and lungs, he could finally breathe. Now that he had all his parts, he could finally breathe.

And then all his parts screamed *danger* to him, *jump* to him, and he jumped.

ꜱ   ꜱ   ꜱ

Later, Penny couldn't describe what happened to her. She wasn't supposed to, anyway, but she wanted to. She wanted to tell her father. He'd never graduated—he'd moved to town too late, after he was in high school—and Penny, more than anything, wanted to tell him why she felt different about him after that day.

But how do you say to your father, I know now how it feels. I know now, really know, why, after your accident you couldn't sit home, why you had to take whatever job you could, even if it didn't pay much, even if it meant always being gone. And I know why, when you are home, you can't pay much attention to me because what you have to do, what something is forcing you to do is make sure the furnace works and the roof doesn't leak and the hot water heater can make it through another year. And why when you do pay attention to me you yell because I'm growing up and you're scared I'll grow up too fast and get hurt and you're scared that you won't have money for college and sometimes you almost hate me because I need so much from you that maybe you can't give and you want to give because I'm yours. I'm yours.

But it was so hard to put into words. Because it had nothing to do with words. Penny could see herself, as she'd been that day, flying up as high as she could get, perching up as high as she could get and bursting out with . . . what? Challenge? Invitation? Not holding anything back, declaring herself? himself? Ready to fight, ready to die, even, for the chance to move the life *inside*, out. Out to connect, to be born again, born on and on and on, forever.

And she could have died. She never saw Mr. Heinman after that day without wishing she could tell him, too. Because the challenge she'd issued hadn't been ignored. The territory she'd claimed had been defended. She'd had to throw her new red dress away after that day, and she would always have to wear her hair long to hide the scars on the back of her neck.

ↆ   ↆ   ↆ

I'll show you who can believe. At first it was Tim's only thought. Over and over it hammered at him as he sat, his eyes squeezed shut, his hands clenched on his lap into fists. Believe. Okay. But believe what? Believe that I'll turn into a brook trout? No, that's what *she* wants. What do *I* want? What do I *need*?

Power, he thought. To be invisible. To lie hidden and flick into sight, silent, controlled and deadly. To strike, without warning. Not to be afraid of anything, to just reach out with every part of me and take what I want. To have that be okay, not bad, not good, just . . . okay.

He sighed and unclenched. So great, he thought, relaxing. So great . . . And then, so slowly he almost didn't realize it, every part of him was fusing into one part, and then he was lying against the earth, cool against the cool ground, still. Still for a long, dim time. And then somewhere in the dimness, something gleamed. Something blinked.

A gleam, a blink, and then movement, a jump, and it was something he wanted, something he needed, something he couldn't let get away. And suddenly he was uncoiling, reaching out toward it in one long smooth movement. He was reaching out to feed.

And then? And then Tim found himself on his hands and knees vomiting over the edge of the embankment. He felt a touch on his back and then a handkerchief gently wiping his mouth. He sat back, shivering for a long moment before he could speak.

"I wanted it," he said. "I wanted it so bad, but it was wrong. . . ."

"What was wrong, Tim?" Miss Clough's voice was quiet, and he wanted to burrow against her, to hold onto her and have her understand what he had to tell her without words. But instead he crawled to his feet and sat wearily down on a rock.

"I don't know," he said. "It was right, most of it." He touched his top lip with his tongue. "It . . . smelled right." He glanced at her and then away. "I didn't want to be a trout. I couldn't *believe* in a trout."

Miss Clough was leaning heavily on her stick. Slowly she lowered herself and sat down beside him. "So you took your first choice. Yes. I see. Do you know what Eddy was, Tim? I warned him about water, snakes, but I never thought— Did you think, Tim? Did you think what Eddy had to be?"

Something smooth and green seemed to twitch in front of Tim's eyes and then leap away. He swallowed. "I was so hungry. I wanted it so bad. But then I didn't. It was like I should want it, but there was something wrong and I couldn't . . . But I almost did. I almost . . ." He swallowed again, harder. "Was that . . . Eddy?"

"I don't know," she said. "I wasn't there."

"I was," said Tim. Then he was sick again, knowing for sure what he had almost done. And after, when she reached a comforting arm around him, he didn't pull away.

ᐳ   ᐳ   ᐳ

Mary Margaret didn't close her eyes. She did, however, half close her ears. She could hear Miss Clough's voice but not her words. Miss Clough's words earlier, the story about Mr. Heinman, had upset her just a little. She didn't know why. But it was all right now. Mr. Heinman didn't have anything to do with her, she knew that now. No one had anything to do with her. She was calm again, clear in her mind about what she was going to do.

And she wasn't afraid. Because she'd done it before, of course. At least part of it. Last fall, all alone. It had been scary then, scary until it happened. Until her need had made it happen. And then? A small smile flickered across Mary Margaret's face. And then? And then, the way it had felt had made coming back the hardest thing she'd ever done.

So today would be easy. Because she didn't just believe. She knew. And her choice, her first choice, her only choice, had been right. It had been everything she'd longed for. Since then, every evening she could get away, she'd watched the swallows dart and wheel over the pond and remembered. Remembered how it was to be free.

And it wasn't a sin. It *wasn't*. She wasn't going to die. She was going to live, be something, be her very own self for the very first time. Joey—but she wouldn't think about Joey. Joey would be okay. Joey would have to be okay.

She touched the grass with her fingers. She smelled the lilacs and looked at the poplars moving in the breeze. She listened for one long moment to a cardinal perched somewhere out of sight, singing its heart out. And then she closed her eyes, sank down inside herself, and disappeared.

Nine

IT WAS THREE-FIFTEEN. THE DAY, STILL cool, was brighter now, the sun almost breaking through the haze, and there was a breeze again on the water. Becky sat, her back against one of the poplars, a half-eaten sandwich on the ground beside her. She was fingering the object Miss Clough had given back to her through its thin wrapping. It was one of Billy's cars, the one she'd bought for him with her own money on his first birthday.

She felt . . . She didn't know how she felt. She felt . . . graduated. Partly, deep inside her, was a pinpoint of something so intense it would never, as long as she lived, completely dim. Flying. She knew what flying meant now and she would never forget.

But what she also felt wasn't exciting at all. It was a kind of silence. She felt . . . in layers, if that made any sense, like petals on a flower, each separate but all connected to a central . . . what? She wasn't very good in science. Miss Clough would know.

Then she shook out of herself. Penny was coming toward her. She was a mess. Her lipstick was gone, and most of one sleeve of her dress was torn to shreds. Two of her fingernails were broken, and her hair stuck up in clumps. "Penny! Are you okay?"

"Yeah," said Penny. She plumped herself down beside Becky and smiled. "But I guess it was good that it turned three when it did." She looked up. "You can't see him, but there's one real tough cardinal up there, and this section of creek belongs to him. But you know what? I think I gave him a run for his money. I think I really did."

"But, look!" said Becky. "You're bleeding. Your neck is bleeding!" The cardinals had frightened her earlier because of what they could do to her. But it hadn't been her. Of course not. It had been Penny. She should have been afraid *for* Penny, not *of* Penny. Now, though, she could see neither fear had been necessary. Penny was strong and Penny was her friend.

"It's okay," said Penny. "It doesn't matter. You know, Beck? I feel different. I just really feel different."

Becky nodded. A lot of things would feel different after today. She noticed, without surprise, that Tim and Eddy were sitting together on the embankment, poking holes into the dirt with twigs. They were mostly quiet, but once in a while Eddy would say something to Tim or Tim would say something to Eddy. They'd never had anything to say to each other before today. Now it looked like they did.

But something else was different too. Something not so good that stirred an uneasy memory up out of Becky's calm. "Mary Margaret," she said. "She's not back yet."

"Isn't she?" said Penny. "Well, I was later than you guys. She just must have set her clock a little late. Becky?"

Becky had stood up. She found she ached in odd places. Her shoulders were sore, and her toes hurt. For a minute she wasn't sure she could walk, but she could. Or at least hobble. "Miss Clough?" she said when she finally got to the bench. "Miss Clough?"

The teacher slowly opened her eyes and slowly focused. "Becky," she said. "Sit down." Gingerly, Becky sat.

"Miss Clough, Mary Margaret's not back yet."

"I'm afraid I was dozing," said Miss Clough. "What time is it?"

The uneasy feeling grew. Miss Clough didn't doze. Miss Clough always knew what time it was. "It's three-thirty," she said. "Mary Margaret should be back by now."

Miss Clough hardly seemed to hear her. She was looking over at Tim and Eddy. "They might be able to be friends now," she said. "I was worried about Tim, you know. He'd been torn loose from so much. If he refused to graduate, I was afraid that he'd never connect again. But now I think he will. You've helped him, Becky."

Yes, Becky thought, with a warm surge of

pride. I did help, at least a little. And maybe he'll never . . . like me, like he does Penny. But at least now he knows who I am.

"Thank you," she said shyly, and then she remembered. "But Miss Clough. Mary Margaret. I'm worried about her. She was talking funny, earlier, and she looked funny, too."

"Funny?" said Miss Clough, but she turned to Becky and finally seemed to be listening.

Becky spoke slowly, trying to be clear about the picture she'd seen and the expression on the martyr's face. And the expression she'd seen on Mary Margaret's face that morning, and what she'd said. "She kept talking about sin, about being bad. . . ."

Miss Clough's answer sounded rehearsed, as though her words were ones she'd often repeated to herself. "I've seen so many girls like Mary Margaret over the years, farm girls with too many brothers and sisters, too many responsibilities. Too little childhood. But they survive, and later things are actually easier for them, because—"

"Miss Clough," said Becky, and then she knew that she really was different. She never would have dared interrupt Miss Clough before. "Please, Miss Clough. Listen. I think she's been here before. I think she came down here last fall. That was the bad thing she was talking about, coming down here and . . . graduating all by herself. So this time . . . this time, maybe it's like what people do sometimes. 'Going through the gate.' And then never . . . then never coming back."

Now Miss Clough's hooded black eyes were staring right into Becky's face. "You feel she was that unhappy? *That* unhappy, Becky?"

Finally Becky was able to put what she felt into words, what she'd been trying this past year to understand about Mary Margaret. "I think she didn't feel she . . . mattered. Except as somebody to take care of everybody else. It was like she was invisible, so nobody really knew her because she wasn't really there. I think she felt like . . . nothing."

Like I thought I felt, she realized suddenly. But for Mary Margaret it was real. That's how life really was. A wave of shame washed over her.

Beside her there was a terrible silence. Then Miss Clough spoke. "Then I'm a fool," she said. "A blind old fool who has no business still teaching. I let her have her first choice."

Something cold washed over Becky. "What do you mean?"

"Her first choice," said Miss Clough and dragged herself upright with her stick. "I never let students have their first choice. It's too dangerous. But I was taken in by what she said, because Mary Margaret was always so adult and responsible. So very responsible."

Penny had come over and was tugging at Becky's arm. "What's the matter? What's wrong?" But Becky couldn't answer.

Now Eddy and Tim were there, too. "You okay, Miss Clough?" said Eddy. Becky noticed vaguely that he sounded more sure of himself. He seemed to fit himself somehow, and he wasn't blinking.

But that wasn't important now. "Why is it dangerous, Miss Clough?" she said. She could hardly breathe.

"Tim could tell you one reason," said Miss Clough. "Why a first choice can be dangerous. If it upsets the balance. If it's a predator, when another of you has chosen to be prey. I was blind there too, not seeing that someone might disobey. Eddy only escaped because Tim was stronger and more human than he knew. But the other reason . . ."

She swayed, and terrified, Becky grabbed her arm. Then she saw Eddy had her other arm and together they eased the old woman back onto the bench. Miss Clough shook them off. "The other reason is that your first choice is what you really want to be. You want it too much. And if you want it too much, too much of you can sink down into it, and there's not enough of you left."

"Not enough for what?" cried Penny.

Miss Clough smiled bitterly. "*To* what, Penny. There's not enough left of you to come back." They all stood as though turned to stone, but Miss Clough ignored them. Her eyes were sunk far back in her head and her gaze, too, was inward.

"And I didn't know. I didn't know she wanted it too much. Because she'd chosen swallow, you see. She said she'd chosen it because she really didn't know what to be and I talked a lot about swallows, I seemed to like swallows. She said she really didn't care, but swallows were the one thing she could watch because they came to her pond, and that would help because she was so busy. 'If that's okay with you, Miss Clough. If that's okay with you.' "

Suddenly she looked up, her eyes terrifying. "And yes, of course, of course it was okay. Because I was flattered that someone had finally chosen swallow after all these years. And because I really didn't care. I was worried about someone else, and I really didn't care enough about Mary Margaret to know who she was."

"But you'll get her back, Miss Clough," said Eddy. "You . . ." He stepped back as though seeing something in her face he'd never seen before. "At least . . ."

"I will always bring you back," said Miss Clough slowly. "And I thought I could, one last time. One last class. Surely, I thought, I had the strength to graduate one last class. But now?"

"But now what?" said Becky. "Please, Miss Clough! Please! You have to bring Mary Margaret back. You have to!"

Slowly Miss Clough raised her head. She looked at each of them for a long moment, first Penny, then Eddy, then Tim, and finally Becky. A faint smile flickered over her face.

"I can't," she said. "Not now. Not anymore. But you can."

Ten

SHE LOOKED SHRUNKEN NOW, FLIMSY, LIKE
the tattered Raggedy Ann Becky still propped
against the post of her bed. Only her eyes still
gleamed with life as they moved from one frightened face to the next. "You can, you know. Now
you've graduated. But you must hurry. The more
time she's there, the harder it will be for her
to . . . hear you." She fumbled in the basket beside
her and pulled something out. "This might help.
But if what Becky feels is true, maybe not."

She handed it to Becky, and Becky, petrified,
saw that everyone had turned toward her, was looking at her as though she knew what to do. She had
no idea what to do except unwrap the tiny pack-

age. It wasn't really even a package, just something rolled up inside a Kleenex and fastened with a rubber band. But the band had been wound again and again, wound as firmly as the band around the end of tightly braided hair. Like Bridget's hair, wispy hair that came undone by the end of every morning, and that Mary Margaret reworked every lunch hour into new perfect braids.

"Let me try," said Penny. "I've still got a couple of fingernails left." In a few seconds she'd worked the first turn loose. Quickly she unwound it and then handed it back to Becky. "You unwrap it, Beck," she said. "You'll know what it means."

At first Becky didn't know what it meant at all. Because inside the Kleenex was another one, and inside that? Becky shook it out and then shook it out again. There was nothing there. Then she understood.

"Wait a minute," said Tim. "Wait a minute."

But Becky didn't. With careful deliberation she smoothed out the two tissues and then began to fold them. When they were as small as she could get them she wound them up again with the rubberband. Then she turned and threw the tiny bundle as hard as she could under the bank of lilacs. She let a long shuddering breath out into the silence.

"Mary Margaret didn't leave it to help her come back," she said. "She left it empty so she wouldn't come back." Becky looked at her friends fiercely. "But we're going to bring her back. Because it wasn't just Miss Clough that didn't . . . care enough. I didn't care either. I never even tried to help her."

"I didn't either," said Penny. "I just thought she was playing . . . you know, being the little mother, like that made her more important than anybody else."

"I thought she liked it," said Eddy. "I thought she liked them." Then he shook his head, as though reminding himself of something he wasn't quite used to yet. "Feelings are as important as other stuff. You should name them right. I thought she . . . loved them."

"She did," said Tim gruffly. "But you can . . . love people and hate them, too. She always scared me, because— Well, it doesn't matter why. But if she doesn't come back, well, then, we didn't really graduate, did we? Like you said before," he said to Becky, "we've got to have everybody, or it's no good."

"Miss Clough?" said Becky. "We can call her back, can't we? If we care enough?"

"If you care enough," said Miss Clough. "But hurry. Get as close to the creek as you can. And then find Mary Margaret inside of you. Find good memories for her. Find the things she loves, things powerful enough to reach her. Find . . ." But then her face froze. She closed her eyes. "I can't . . ." she whispered, and then began to breathe like an animal caught in a trap.

"Miss Clough?" said Eddy. "Miss Clough?" He looked from the silent shaking figure to Becky. "She's sick. I knew there was something wrong all this spring but I didn't know how to . . . It's all right, Miss Clough. We'll help you. We'll get help!"

"Eddy, we can't!" said Becky. Her own face was almost as white as Miss Clough's and she could feel her breath coming in the same shallow gasps. "That's not what she wants. She wants Mary Margaret. You do, Miss Clough, don't you? That's what you want us to do?"

She wasn't sure if Miss Clough had heard her. The teacher's breathing had slowed, and she had sagged back against the tree. Only her hands were moving, clenching and unclenching the black stick that lay across her lap. And then the index finger of her right hand came up and pointed toward the creek.

"Thank you," Becky whispered. She took a deep breath and then another. Then she took Eddy's hand. "We will help her, Eddy. But we have to do this first." She held out her other hand to Penny and then motioned her to do the same to Tim. "It just feels . . . stronger. Come on."

Even as she spoke, they all straightened. Eddy stopped shaking, and the color came back into Penny's face as the confusion left Tim's. Something calm and powerful was moving now from one hand to another, passing from one body into the next. They felt somehow like one person now, not four, and without thinking they all began to move at the same time. They came to the very edge of the embankment and stopped.

They looked for a minute at the creek below.

The light was afternoon light now, lower and clearer. Insects skated along the surface of the pool, their movement intensified here and there by the delicate ripples of fish moving up to feed. On the far bank a blackbird swung gently from a cattail and looked at them without fear. A clump of pussy willows splayed out against the empty sky.

Becky took Penny's hand more securely and then Eddy's and then closed her eyes. Find Mary Margaret. Find what's inside her. Find what she needs here. Find what she loves here. Then reach out to her where she is now, because we can now, because we've been there. And call her back. Call her back.

➘　➘　➘

The swing. Remember the swing, Mary Margaret, and how it feels to pump up, to reach for the tree with your toes and then whoosh back down again. And winter days at recess—I remember you laughing once, sliding down the ice run we made, the only one who got all the way to the fence without falling. And that Halloween Joey dressed up like a pirate, that was your idea, remember, and he felt so big and brave, I'd never seen him like that before, and you were so proud. . . . You were so proud of Joey. . . .

ゝ　　ゝ　　ゝ

I do like you, Mary Margaret. I really do. We can be friends. We'll need each other in junior high. It's going to be scary, but not if we're all there together. And your hair could be so pretty. Your dad will have to let you get it cut in junior high, Mary Margaret. I'll ask my mom to ask him, she's so good with hair, it'll look so cute. Junior high, Mary Margaret! Things will be different then. You won't have the kids all day. I mean, I know you love them, but watching them every minute must be hard, and next year, next year, well, it will just be you. Just you, Mary Margaret, with us, your friends. And the kids will be okay. It'll be good for Joey, being the biggest, he'll do so good, Joey, the big brother, you'll be so proud of him. . . .

ゝ　　ゝ　　ゝ

You're really smart, Mary Margaret. You remember that project you did on moths? You had stuff in there I couldn't do, the way you saw so much about them, not just the surface stuff, but what it means. Nobody else did that. Not even me. Not then. And you know what it's like to get into, really get into some of those books Miss Clough has. I've seen you reading them, and it wasn't fair you didn't have more time, but you will next year, that long bus ride, it'll be great for reading, Mary Margaret. And then you can share it with Joey. Joey's a lot like you, Mary Margaret, he's smart, too, and you're lucky you have somebody you can talk to, right in your own family. Somebody you can share things with, who thinks you're great. . . .

➘ ➘ ➘

Look. See, it's no use running away, Mary Margaret. I don't really know you, but I know what you're thinking, you're thinking your dad, your mom, whatever, they don't love you like they do the other ones, the little ones, they just take you for granted. Like, yeah, Mary Margaret, she's bigger, she's older, she can handle it, it's tough, but she'll be okay, we don't have to worry about Mary Margaret. So you're going to show them, right? They'll be sorry, right? Okay, so probably they will, but where does that get you? Nowhere. And Joey. Joey, you know? I talk to Joey sometimes, he's

not a bad kid, but he needs . . . Well, he needs you,
Mary Margaret. Those other kids in your family, well,
they'll make mush out of him, 'cause he's different from
them, just like you. I don't want to make you feel bad,
but you'd better get back here, because if you don't,
well, things are going to be real bad for Joey. . . .

➘   ➘   ➘

Joey. Joey. Joey. Joey. Their thoughts had all
come together now into one word and Becky felt it
toll out of her, toll out of them all like a great bell.
Joey. Joey. Joey. Joey. She opened her eyes. The sky
was no longer empty. A bird had appeared, and although she sometimes had trouble with birds, trouble telling them apart, she didn't with this one. It
was one of the first birds she'd learned, the swallow,
with its long tail, its shape so clear that it looked
cut out of paper like those silhouettes Becky's
grandmother had made that hung now on her bedroom wall.

But this swallow was different. It looked all
right, but its movement wasn't the smooth glide,
the quick dart as it skimmed the water and up
again, that Becky knew so well. This swallow was

flying slowly, beating rather than darting, seeming to stop in midair before it caught itself, and then beating harder so as not to fall.

Mary Margaret, thought Becky, and the others thought with her. Come back, Mary Margaret. We need you. Miss Clough needs you. Joey needs you. Oh, Joey, Mary Margaret. Joey needs you.

Again the swallow faltered. For a minute it beat more strongly, moving up, moving away, but then it circled back down. Down it came to the very surface of the pool and then with a terrible effort back up again. This time its circle was lower, its beat slower. It hesitated and then sank like a stone into the water.

"Come on!" yelled Eddy, and Becky felt her arm almost yanked out of its socket. Now they were sliding, falling, catching on tree roots and scraping elbows against rocks, until finally they had scrambled down to the very edge of the creek. Something was roiling in the pool, coming to the surface like a huge trout and then going back under.

"She can't swim!" Becky screamed. "She doesn't know how to swim!" Tim was already cursing at his shoes, clawing at the laces, hauling them off and throwing them back up on the rocks. But Eddy was ahead of him. As Tim dove in Eddy had already pushed himself with powerful kicks out into the center of the pool and then down.

Mary Margaret came up again, her hair like weeds against the water. Her hand grabbed for the sky and then fell. And then Eddy came up under her, pushing her head up and out, and then Tim was there, grabbing her legs.

"Hold onto that root!" Penny yelled to Becky, and taking Becky's other hand, she stepped onto the slippery shelf of rock that hung two feet down under the water. It had been a cool May, and the water was still icy, numbing. She stumbled and then grabbed Becky more firmly. She bent over as far as she could and held out her hand.

"Mary Margaret!" she called. "Come on, Mary Margaret!" and reached for her just as Eddy let go. He clung, gray-faced, to the bank, and Penny grabbed a wad of Mary Margaret's blouse and pulled with all her might. Grunting, Tim swung her legs up and onto the rocks and then crawled out himself.

"I got her," he panted, and as Penny let go, he grabbed Mary Margaret under the arms and swung the rest of her up and out. Penny, dropping Becky's hand, hauled herself out onto her hands and knees and reached down toward Eddy. Then Becky was beside her, and clumsy, struggling, they tugged the upper half of him up and over the shelf of rock and out of the water.

"I'm okay," he grunted. "Just get out of my way." For a few seconds they all lay splayed out against the rocky bank, breathing hard. Then Becky crawled over to where Tim was crouched over Mary Margaret.

"Is she okay?" she said, fighting tears. "Mary Margaret, are you okay?"

Tim looked up at her, his face twisted.

"I don't think she's breathing," he said. "I think maybe she's dead."

Eleven

BUT MARY MARGARET WASN'T DEAD. EVEN as they spoke, she choked, and a dribble of water came out of her mouth.

"Turn her over," said Penny. She had crawled over, too. Her voice was shaky but confident. "I saw it on TV. Turn her over and push the water out. Here. Help me." Together they pushed and tugged Mary Margaret over onto her side. What looked like a whole creekful of water suddenly spewed out her mouth and nose. And then Mary Margaret was coughing and gagging and her eyes opened and she was looking up into Becky's face.

Her gaze slowly cleared. "Becky?" she whispered.

"Oh, Mary Margaret," said Becky.

"Cold," whispered Mary Margaret. "So cold."

"We've got to get her out of here," said Tim. He was shivering, and Eddy's face was splotched with blue. "We've all got to get out of here. Mary Margaret, can you move? Can you get up?"

Mary Margaret groaned.

Becky looked anxiously at the bank above them. It was too steep to carry Mary Margaret up, even if they were strong enough to do it.

"You have to keep moving," said Penny. "That's what they said on TV, so you don't get hypo-something-or-other. Listen. I'm going for help. Eddy, you come with me. You've got a key to the school. We can call the Rescue Squad, and there's lots of dress-up clothes and stuff we can get. They'll be warm. It won't take long. Will you guys be okay?"

Becky looked at her friend gratefully. Penny's bossiness sometimes bugged her, but now it was just what they all needed. She nodded. Penny went on. "You're still dry, Beck. Take off all of Mary Margaret's wet stuff on top and put your flannel shirt on her, okay?" Then she saw the look on Becky's face and sighed with all her old exasperation. "Honestly, Beck. You can do that, can't you? Tim'll look the other way, won't you, Tim? Come on, Eddy."

"Penny?" said Becky. "Will you tell Miss Clough that Mary Margaret's okay?" She wasn't sure how to say what she really wanted to say. Find out if Miss Clough's okay, too. Find out if she's still . . . there.

Penny nodded impatiently, and in another minute she and Eddy had scrambled up the rocky slope and over the top of the embankment.

Mary Margaret was struggling to sit up. Her hair hung over her face, and she pushed it back weakly with both hands. Then she put her hands over her face and burst into tears. She cried in struggling coughing sobs that wrenched up out of her as if she'd never cried before.

Finally she became quieter and lifted her face, blotchy with misery, up to Becky's. "I did want to die. I didn't know. But that's what I wanted, the most terrible sin there is. Why didn't you let me?"

It was hard to say, because even now Becky wasn't sure if it was true. But it was true enough.

"We love you, Mary Margaret," she said. But Mary Margaret shook her head.

"Nobody loves me," she said. "Not even God. Not anymore."

Tim cleared his throat. "Joey . . ." he started. "He . . . Joey does. You know he does. And us . . . well, if you hadn't come back, it sure would have screwed up graduation."

Mary Margaret was silent. Then she shivered. "I'm cold," she said.

"Here," said Becky and started to take off her flannel shirt.

"Listen," said Tim. "She's okay, isn't she? And I'm freezing, too. I'm going up with those other guys, okay?"

Becky didn't know if she felt relieved or disappointed. But she knew now that he wasn't going because he hated her or because she was just a boring nobody. It didn't have anything to do with her. He was just tired and cold and needed to get moving.

"Here's one of your shoes," she said. "And I think I see the other one up on that rock."

"Thanks," he said. He began picking his way

upward, wincing at the roots and stones under his thin socks.

Becky helped Mary Margaret out of her blouse and T-shirt and into the heavy flannel. "It's good I'm fatter than you are," she said, wishing she didn't feel so awkward. "I can see me trying to get into your stuff."

A little color had come back into Mary Margaret's face. "Where's Miss Clough? How come she isn't here? She hates me, doesn't she? Now she really hates me."

Becky felt like shaking her. Here they'd all saved her life and she wasn't even grateful. All she could talk about was how everybody hated her. But that's how she *feels*. The thought jolted Becky, just as it had earlier. That's how Mary Margaret feels and has always felt. Now she was just naming it. And like Eddy said, naming things right is good. Especially when you've never done it before.

"Miss Clough's sick," she said. "I think she's been sick for a long time. She couldn't bring you back, but she told us how." And now she knew she'd have to name something, too. "Mary Margaret, I never knew you felt the way you did. I didn't want to know things were so crummy for you. I didn't try. I'm sorry. I'm really sorry."

Mary Margaret was crying again. But her tears were calmer now, and when she finally stopped it was as if something hard and ugly had melted and drained out of her. She stared down at her hands. "I thought I'd feel free. I did, last time. But this time, I just felt . . . alone. They didn't care, either, the swallows." Then she looked up at Becky from out of the tangle of her hair. "Becky, could you . . . do you think . . . could you . . . be my friend?"

Becky nodded violently, wiping away her own tears with both hands. She felt like she'd been crying all day. "I'll be your friend, Mary Margaret."

Mary Margaret gave a deep sigh. Then she sat up straighter and pushed the hair out of her face. "I hate my hair," she said suddenly, sounding so unlike herself and like Penny that Becky almost laughed.

"I'll bet your dad will let you cut it now, now you've graduated."

Mary Margaret looked puzzled. "We did, didn't we? We graduated." They sat quietly for a minute, and then Mary Margaret struggled to her feet. "I want Joey," she said. "Can you help me get up there, Becky? I think I can do it."

"Okay," said Becky. She stood up quickly. Miss Clough, she thought. I want to see Miss Clough. She felt stiff, and damp from the rocks. "You go first and I'll kind of push at you from behind if you need it."

They went up slowly but without much trouble. The bank was steep but there were a lot of places to hold on. It felt good to move, even though Becky was feeling more and more scared about what she'd find at the top.

But when they finally pulled themselves over the edge, what they saw was Penny and Tim running toward them. Penny was lugging a pile of dress-up clothes, and Tim had a rope.

"Hey, you're up!" called Penny. "That's great! Here, Mary Margaret. Here's the witch's cape. Or would you rather be Superman?"

Mary Margaret looked at the two capes seriously. "I think I'll be a witch," she finally said and pulled the black one around her. It made her look much older, older and somehow dignified. She hesitated, opened her mouth as if to say something and then stopped. Her eyes filled again with tears.

"It's okay," said Penny, and Tim nodded.

Mary Margaret turned again to Becky. "I want Joey," she said.

"We'll take her up," said Penny. "Becky, could you stay with Miss Clough? The school phone wasn't working, so Eddy had to go over to the parsonage to call the Rescue. But they should be here fast."

Even after all they'd been through, Penny was glowing with energy. Becky had a sudden flash of her in the future, a principal in some big school, or the head of some big company, ordering everybody around. But that was okay. Somebody had to be boss. And she knew now that she could do something Penny couldn't do. She could listen to people. She could begin to understand them. She could even talk to them. And the person she most wanted to talk to now was Miss Clough.

Miss Clough was still sitting on the bench, still leaning back against the poplar. Her eyes were closed, but one finger was moving slowly, going round and round the knob at the end of her stick.

Becky stood for a minute looking down at her. Why hadn't she noticed how thin Miss Clough had gotten? How pale? Because she'd never really looked at grown-ups before. She'd never really looked at anything before today.

"Miss Clough," she said softly. "Are you okay?"

Miss Clough opened her eyes. "Becky," she said. Becky sat down on the bench beside her. She still wasn't quite sure what she wanted to say, so she reached down and after a brief struggle pulled off her muddy shoes and socks. She waited until an ant had crawled out of the way and then wiggled her toes deep into the soft grass. It felt wonderful.

"Miss Clough," she said. "Is there any reason why the grass is the way it is? Why this place is?"

"I don't know for sure," said Miss Clough haltingly. "I've thought about it often, of course, and what I've decided, maybe, is that it's a place that just somehow was given more *life*. As though a current, a connection is stronger here so that it has a kind of energy that could do almost anything. You feel it, don't you?" Becky nodded.

"There must be other spots like it," Miss Clough went on, "but I think, I've come to think, that it isn't enough just for a place like this to be. Someone has to recognize it. Claim it. Use it. Like a gardener recognizes the place that will allow a particular plant to grow into what it was really meant to be. So that's what I did. I recognized this place, and I claimed it. I claimed it for us." She looked steadily at Becky. "And when I'm gone, someone will claim it again. Not right away, maybe. But someday, I'm sure of that. Because this is our place."

"Our place," Becky breathed. Yes. That was right. Our place. She watched Miss Clough's finger. Round and round. Round and round. "What's your stick say? That writing?"

"Greek," said Miss Clough. "A . . . summing up, my father said, from the writings of Hippocrates. This was his stick, my father's. He was a doctor, and he carved the letters himself so he wouldn't forget. I thought it was just as important for a teacher. 'First, do no harm,' it says." She spoke now as though every word was being pulled out of her, painfully. "I didn't do a very good job, did I?"

"Yes, you did," Becky said fiercely. "For years and years and years. It's just that you're sick now.

But, Miss Clough? I don't want you to be sick. I want you to get better. Can't you get better?"

"In my pocket," whispered Miss Clough. "Sweater." Becky looked. The left sweater pocket was empty, but in the right one she found a small white envelope.

"Pill," whispered Miss Clough. "Two . . ."

Becky fumbled out two small white pills. "Should I . . . ?" she said awkwardly.

"Please," said Miss Clough and Becky fed her first one and then the other. Miss Clough worked them slowly down. "Thank you," she said finally, and the grip on her stick relaxed. "Thank you. I won't die just this minute, you know. Dr. Philpot needs to torture me a little bit first. I owe him that. Although of course I was tempted . . ."

Becky waited. All she wanted was for Miss Clough to keep talking. To keep . . . alive.

Miss Clough was sitting up a bit straighter, and she looked out now over the creek. "So tempted to just go . . . 'through the gate.' It would save such a lot of bother. I wouldn't last long, among the swallows. But Mary Margaret won't let me now, will she? She taught me how wrong it would be."

"Mary Margaret said that, too," said Becky. "That it was a sin. That God would hate her."

Miss Clough shook her head wearily. "It's not in God's nature to hate. I don't know, Becky. What is sin? Hurting others deliberately, yes. Hurting yourself. And maybe nothing hurts you more than going against what God meant for you. Trying to escape what you are. And what I am is human. It's been wonderful to connect with all that other life out there. We're all . . . so much richer because of that. But in the end, in the end, I'm not a swallow, am I? I'm . . . well, what?" She smiled faintly. "What am I, Becky?"

Becky was crying again. "You're our teacher, Miss Clough. And if you're sick . . . gone . . . the school will close and nothing will ever be the same. And Billy . . . Oh, Miss Clough, if you're not here, who's going to help Billy graduate?"

Becky was sure Miss Clough didn't speak. But the voice that echoed now in her head was Miss Clough's voice, Miss Clough's words, Miss Clough's promise. "Someone . . ." Becky heard as clearly as she'd ever heard anything before. ". . . someday, I'm sure of that." And then she felt something heavy and cold being pressed into her hand and looked down. It was the key to the gate.

She looked back up. But Miss Clough had closed her eyes again and leaned back against the tree. Becky sat beside her, her tears slowly drying, her heart slowly quieting. She smelled the lilac and watched the light of late afternoon filter through the trees. And she listened. As she sat, the key held firmly in her hand, she listened to what she'd never heard before. It was the sound of birds calling to each other, and to her. And then came the voices of the Rescue coming down the path.